NEURODATTA

STEFAN TOIO

NEURODATTA

1ª Edição

2022

Stefan Toio

Instagram: @stefan.toio
Twitter: @StefanToio
Email: stefantoio.oficial@gmail.com

Cover Address: Pexels
Cover Author: Mikhail Nilov
Cover photo author's Instagram: @dreamwood.studio
Cover photo author's website: www.dreamwood.pro

The book cover has free usage copyrights as per Pexels website image usage policy with image consumers and image distributors.

Cover design and image alteration: Stefan Toio

Neurodatta: Registered Work / Date: 07/14/2022.

Toio, Stefan

Neurodatta / Stefan Toio. -- 1. ed. -- Alvorada, RS : Ed. do Autor, 2022.

ISBN: 9798845866868
1. Brazilian fiction 2. science-fiction. 3 Cyberpunk. I. Title.

What is the future?

The hope of the past?

Or the failure of the present?

Every advertising sign was hacked, every mobile device, every website and every television station in town. It was not known how it was done, who it was or where it came from. All that, allthat effort for someone to leave just one message...

"They said that in those days evil was strong, it acted in every physical form of being. But today, we are more and more certain that evil acts differently, because we all know, and we don't have the courage to speak out, that today evil reigns by exploiting our subjectivity."

"Do you guys believe in freedom?"

"Or have they been convinced to believe she exists?"

NAKAMURA

A dark room with indirect yellow and blue lights... Someone was there... With sunglasses, right arm bent, pistol pointed upwards, watching with caution, leather pants, grey shirt followed by a leather jacket, black hair a little fallen to the side and shaved on the sides... His eyes shone, lit up like little leds, the blue of the eyeballs were sparkling with excitement that could be seen through the lenses of the glasses... It was him... Commanding the whole thing: — Here... You can put it out. Send them to hell.

Brad: — But Charlie. The guys are just employees of the thing... They have nothing to do with the scheme. They're already tied up; we don't need to do this.

Charlie: — Fuck. Put your finger on this shit. Fuck it up.

A bang was heard, gunshot with a flash and everything. One less to tell the tale that night. It was to be expected, Brad refused to obey, he was the first to die... He was there... His body on the floor with blood coming out of his head and short circuits sparking in the bullet hole.

You could see Ryan nervous with a machine gun and his finger scratching on the trigger: — What do we do with them?

Charlie then grabbed a lighter, lit a cigarette, took a drag and said: — Leave them there. Let's blow this shit up anyway.

They heard those muffled voices, all the employees dressed in orange overalls, tied up, struggling with dread, sitting on the floor with their backs to each other with blindfolds and cloth over their mouths. One even pissed all over himself as the fear was very evident between his shoulders. Nothing could be done. They already knew... Death was certain.

A scream was heard in the corridor. It was Mia, holding the pistol in her hands and the samurai sword on her back watching the door: — What's up... Are you gonna hurry up or are you gonna stay tied up? They're fucking coming up.

Jeniffer crouched down with one knee on the ground finishing setting up the explosives: — Hold on. I'm almost done here.

It was then that they heard Alex on the radio talking from inside the van: — You can start the party. I'm waiting for you down here.

Soon there was dread in Mia's eyes and she quickly closed the emergency door: — We can't handle it... The first batch is coming... Get ready...

Charlie quickly positioned the team by waving the seats: — Ryan... You take the left side... Near the pillar, near the servers, you counter attack... Jeniffer... Set up the high calibers. Stay behind the small wall.

Jeniffer triggering and preparing the machine gun: — It's time to put some assholes in the refrigerator.

The emergency door was closed and a few lights were visible below followed by the sound of boots climbing the stairs. As they climbed the sound of footsteps increased... More rapid footsteps, running, getting louder... Until the light under the door showed someone on the left and someone on the right...

The sound of machine guns adjusting themselves and boots demonstrated the preparation to arrive shooting.

The first guy kicked the door, another two were arriving breaking in, in their first steps Mia propped up beside the door on the wall, she acted quickly with the samurai sword tearing off a couple of legs, the back of one guy and the front of another, followed by a pistol shot to the forehead the second who didn't even know where the bullet   came from... It was evident the red spot in the doorway, it was gushing that surprise blood towards the door, one of them was already dead with a head bullet while the other held his thigh feeling a great pressure of the lost leg, getting in shock and soon he was going to die... The machine gun was already on the ground. He screamed in pain and the third one stepped back saying *"shit"*, and went quickly to shoot just with the gun propped on the wall... But he felt the surprise right away, he couldn't even think straight, cause Jeniffer managed to hit his elbow and all he could see was that arm being ripped against the wall, still with his finger on the trigger, the arm alone machine gunning in the air and then falling on the floor hitting two more guys on the stairs... Mia just put the barrel on the other side of the door and oriented herself through the guy's screams, hitting his forehead... But she had to retreat because near the stairs there were two shots that almost hit her arm.

At that moment the team heard that voice coming from the stairwell... *"Shit happened. We have five dead ... Call fucking backup... We're fucked.* Ryan didn't think twice and came forward and shot the guys in the stairwell... They were shooting in the face, arms, chest, legs, the idea was to unload the comb in the crazy guys ... You could see the guys being shot painting the wall red, as if they didn't want to fall and were enjoying dying. The shooting only stopped when a bullet grazed Ryan's neck and another caught his right shoulder, he fell down and came back crouching... There were two more crazy faggots on the shot and they were going for everything or nothing.

At this moment Charlie became enraged, threw away his cigarette and walked quickly to the door with his pistol pointed upwards: — Fuck! Can't they cool some weak shit like that?

He could see the hastiness of the guys eager to get some shots and finish the job right away... He showed his face on the corner of the door and that lantern light blurred his face, they had five shots in a row on the door when he retreated his face. From there he did the gun weight and trigger time count, at that moment he ended up throwing himself standing right up to the other corner of the wall after the door... When the blast started by the guy in front of him the other one tried to shoot precisely, then Charlie leaned his back on the wall getting well exposed to him, but the gun would take long to get there, he calculated well enough to be free to shoot easily and end up hitting the head of the first guy... When the second guy managed to aim for the wall in front of the door, it was already late, Charlie rolled towards the door and crouched hitting his neck and eye... He got up and went to him in a rage following frantically shooting the corpse while splashing blood on his face: — Take it in the fucking ass. Who do you think you are? Do you think it's okay to take me down?

Just then he came back into the room wiping his face of blood and spoke: — Jeniffer... It's up to you... Mia... The ladder is yours.

Mia turned back to the stairs and saw many more guards coming up... It was a number that couldn't be held back... It was now or never.

Meanwhile Jeniffer was crouching down preparing the explosives: — Now we're done. Finished... All done.

Ryan: — Come on.

Charlie shouted: — Mia!!! Come!!!

They shook suddenly when something caught them by surprise, shuddering where they stood. There was an explosion a few floors below. Mia saw from the stairs some legs ripped off, arms being thrown up, uniforms toast, and the whole thing down there was on fire... Through the window Ryan saw the smoke from the path of the missile launcher coming from that guy at the door of the van. Then they heard on the radio Alex: — It's no use having armored windows if some crazy guy was taking a shit and left one of them open down there... Pay attention... I think they are preparing a third batch. Is everything ready?

Charlie: — All set... We're coming down.

The C4s were prepared. The room was all lit up, the blue leds made the eyes hurt with those yellow dots flashing on the machines. It seemed to be in the doctor's office ready to be seen, but it was the air conditioning with the extreme temperature to avoid the overheating of the servers. An air with the smell of purity and cleanliness to leave the God of the city untouched.... This was no ordinary floor of Nakamura's building... It was the central hub of restricted data of all citizens. Hacked and downloaded with the intent to extort by private messages, hate conversations in closed groups, access to pornos, stalkees, bank movements, corruptions... Everything to have control of future councilors, mayors and anyone who stood in their way.

It was an unusual day, the directors were excited, the prototype worked perfectly... Champagne bubbles popped on the top floor, celebrating the first artificial intelligence capable of real-time scanning for potential dangers to the corporation and producing data to incriminate anyone. After all, you couldn't arrest a machine with a manufacturing defect, their speech was ready in case something leaked.

Then there was the sound of breaking glass, the wind blowing so hard that it pulled out the window, moving Charlie's hair. From above you could see him jumping from the building with his team, deploying the parachute and in the background happening that explosion in the center of the building. Months of work destroyed. Another Nakamura plan thrown down the drain.

Entering the van they celebrated another job done, this one had a different taste, as it directly attacked Nakamura's way of using data. A task that could only be done by a cyber-terrorist forged in the hatred of corporations, forgotten and left by society at the mercy of their wills.

THE BUSINESS

Arriving at NeonDyne, the team was celebrating another day of work done and Neurocoin in the account. It was a place full of gangs, several corners with tables and comfortable chairs, full of black light near the tables, fluorescent lights under the benches, pink and blue neon lights that charmed the dark tables with loaded guns and machine guns... All this in the mixture of the rhythm between the loud sound of heavy rock and the parallel conversations in all corners, cigarette smoke, deals being made, jobs being planned, celebrations of concluded services, open bottles with glasses full of sparkling drinks and some guys snorting drugs to enjoy the rest of the night. Nobody liked to drink sitting down, the business was to stay drinking standing up to tell stories of robbery and death, or talk about the marked cards of murder... It was a hallucinating atmosphere full of excessive self-confidence, unpredictability, nervous shoulders, suspicious remarks... All mingled with the fissure of flickering glances from eye implants, carefree glances, wary stares, and the uncertainty of being experiencing the last day of life. The bar had a yellow led center table all around its edge and dark colored metal high chairs. The deal was simple... Payment all cash, nothing on credit.

For Charlie and his team it was time to take all and puff some drugs sinister until losing consciousness, no drug was as powerful as DeadReeper, felt the steel tearing the flesh, it penetrated all the circuits infiltrated the body changing the electrical functions of the implants in the nervous system, desynchronizing the synaptic openings as if it was acquiring a new memory, pure lucidity in wonderland. The guys had already packed up some crazy shit to finish themselves off and went into the night with everything they had to offer. It was when they approached the central table to order some drinks and the bartender with a chrome prosthetic right arm handing the bottles on the table came saying and nodding her head: — Here Charlie... Looks like there's someone waiting for you.

— Really?

She propped both hands on the table, looked at that lonely guy at the end of the table, and then looked at Charlie: — He's been here for a while now.

Charlie looked at this guy in dark glasses and a suit in a place like this, full of gangs armed to the teeth, he was suspicious, with no exposed steel and no tattoos to show he was a gang member. Then his eyes shone, he transferred the Neurocoin, picked up the bottle, took a sip: — Alright. I'll go see what it is.

Charlie, holding the bottle with his right hand, adjusted the high stool with his left hand and sat next to the guy who stood out in the crowd: — Hey... They told me you're looking for me.

— I'm here at the request of my boss... He wants to hire your services...

— Okay. Let's talk... You start by telling me who your boss is. I'll find him tomorrow so we can talk... What do you think? Today is a day for celebration.

— He is someone who, let's say, is quite reserved, he likes his work to be done quietly, without fanfare, without becoming barroom gossip. Mr. Charlie... He insists on today.

— Can't you tell me now what the job would be?

— He insists on speaking with you personally... And I can assure you that the payment will be very rewarding.

— Okay. Hold on a second.

Charlie approached his team and asked: — Jeniffer. Have you seen that guy anywhere?

Jeniffer then zoomed in on her eyes that sparkled as she scanned them cautiously: — No. But look above her hands. Do you see that line that looks like the number one with the square almost closing? It's a special series. Custom made for security guards to protect themselves from bullets... Better yet... Giving up their body to protect someone.

— What do you think?

— These models come without serial number to not be tracked while wandering around, it is difficult to act with a Neuroconnection direct command, it will not act with bioelectric interference in the central system. That's right. Sounds like someone from the government. And the way that model was laid out, he's working for someone strong.

— You vouch for me?

— I know this model. A partner already trampo with a security guard like that doing a job on the side, introduced me to him, I met the guy at a party, he told me all about the Q1aY models that serve to make the guy throw himself in front of a bullet for someone, are normally used in androids that do acid cleaning work in factories thermoelectric bullets. He told me you only have that steel while you're working with them When you get fired, they modify it. I don't know how they do it. But it must be some kind of carnage. If he has this model. He's working for someone in the government.

— All right. I'll go then.

Jeniffer touched Charlie's arm, looking between his hair: —Charlie. Be careful.

— You got it.

Jeniffer: — Anything at all let us know.

Charlie: — I'll leave the tracker on... Anything you guys come get me.

The way to the client, inside the car, through the open window I could feel that air. The smell of violence, corruption and thirst for power... The waking night... Once again sunk in technological junk, mechanical remains and electronic components implanted in those who believed in the future. Purple neons perpassing above the bridges paths, yellow lights dividing the streets sidewalks, orange lights demarcating the pedestrian lanes, red neons showing the traffic paths, the whites of the poles that illuminated the city were thin to the point of showing a trail on the asphalt. Black lights in front of some commercial points painted the glistening whites of the shirts, colored lipsticks, painted eyelashes, scratches detached from the enhancements, appearance of shiny reflections on the chromed prostheses, hair of various colors and styles.

All this was followed by electronic advertising boards on every corner... Everything was sold, from noodles on the street to a sign with an arrow signaling new eyes, different arms, extrasensitive skin systems, face shapes and custom implants. Interactive holograms on buildings and sidewalks gave motion in a society that lived hurriedly under the technological time trance. While the lights showed the beauties of unbridled consumption before relationships and a world full of good emotions... The darkness was darker than one could imagine, one could see only the twinkling eyes and some small points of light from implants in the purest survival of the lack of illumination. Demonstrating streets filled with loneliness, suffering and bodies made like vegetables by the addiction to DeadReeper. It was hard to face the truth and see the glazed looks, serious of aggression and defense by those who lived on the dark side of the night around the reality of which surrounded the alleys and corners with gangs ready for all or nothing ... It was the now... Do you have it or not? If it had a gun, good... If not... Death for sure.

Streets full of death stories that were not known the real reasons, were just stories and speculation circulating in another day in Tech City... One more famous guy, killed someone or died by bullets... They were stories... Stories that caused a shock of reality transmuting and breaking the sensations of lucids in the individualisms addicted to unrealities of alternative worlds.

Simultaneous translations showed the ethnically mixed sidewalks, watched by private cameras of groups of residents, which were observed and hacked by companies. The companies showed their power with tall illuminated buildings, out of tune with the landscape, and just below the loyal consumers with their steel prosthetic body parts and cybernetic implants. He felt obliged to be in front. Performance and improvement were the ball of the game in the performance society.

Decentralized technologies and gangs strengthened private protection, every family was worthy of having weapons to protect themselves, where prosthetics had to match personal style, weapons were homemade items to the point where sellers talked about them matching the tastes of personal implants. Aesthetics were pure enhancement, mechanically modifying your face to look the way you prefer... Nobody laughed, nobody found strange, everything was common, everything was normal, because the steel and the chrome were there... Behind every set of skin... Behind every behavior, behind every action, behind every will, behind every belief, behind performance, behind each and every soul lost in Tech City.

As he looked out the window, he could hear the radio broadcasting the day's news... An ordinary day in Tech City...

Radio. "Hello Tech City... Another night with stories to tell. Hopefully better than last night, where a cybermaniac suddenly attacked twenty two people in Northwire... Forensics has yet to report the real reason behind the unknown man's sword attacks, but all indications are that he mysteriously had a short circuit in his central nervous system that altered his behavior... Again a surprise event with free deaths in another stalled story that the Tech City police can't figure out... In Southbash gang conflict has broken out again, with over four hundred and fifty shootings on one corner... The famous Cloudhub corner... I don't know who's stirred up the hornet's nest, I just know it's not gonna stop. But nobody's gonna be scared. Cloudhub has its main attraction tonight with a full house... It will have the participation of nobody more, nobody less than LineBios in one more electrifying night to the sound of the guitars... It's people... Tonight we'll have punks armed to the teeth, ready to fight back if the confrontation between gangs happens again on the corner of Cloudhub.

From behind the mirror of reality, under the neon painted picture of the city he could see from inside the car the dark corners with subgroups talking at night, cigarette smokes, solitary lights individualized in the wills of each one to have their own improvement. From nowhere you could hear a whistle echoing in the silence, hidden weapons to not give advantage to the competition, loose laughter of self-confidence in the unpredictability of the night, followed by fear hidden in its purest wild will to survive... Sometimes we could see a motorcycle or two arriving in some groups... Even cars approaching and that guy arriving calmly talking to someone inside in the lowered window... Everybody knew... but we didn't know when... or where... Something was going to happen... It wouldn't come with warning... It would come by surprise... Without saying why... Without knowing where it came from.

Amidst all the nightly preparations of the city Charlie was once again focusing on the informative music of the Tech City news...

Radio. "This morning Sidewest returned to normal routine after last night had disrupted the Cybernet system. No Neurocoin remained in circulation and some clouds had been cleared.... Data was out of circulation, personal systems crashed, there was a widespread crash in implants and enhancements... Up to now the

Cybertrack department has not informed what happened and is still checking what happened to the local network... In politics, Mayor Jones is still leading in his re- election bid by fifty-five percent, compared to his opponent Roy... We will have a hot and challenging election. But many voters believe in Jones' idea... Who's against privatizing the police, in favor of more decentralized Cybernet, extending it to microgrids instead of being housed in neighborhoods. And he wants to bring in more Gitstorm companies, to have more competition in the market for neuroclouds and mindpacks."

***

Arriving at the apartment, Charlie was faced with a large room, inside if had a large white leather armchairs facing the balcony, in a room filled with large windows and bar table at the bottom, you could see the life in motion in the city lights circulating down there. Soon after he arrived the security guard said: — You can sit there. He's coming.

As he sat in front he saw that guy on the balcony talking by pingsound, where the fingerprint was interconnected directly with the ear. Walking back and forth, as if he was worried about something... That's when he realized he was in Mayor Jones' apartment. Pictures with his family on the wall, followed by party flyers on the tables, the mix between leisure and work on the top floor of the most expensive building in Tech City. Calling someone at a time like this was surely a very hot stop and needed urgency.

Charlie thought to himself, "Do these suckers still believe that? And don't they realize that freedom is an illusion? What this guy wants doing business this time? It is not enough to manipulate the population gaining from the suffering of others ... If I'd known death and suffering was a lucrative business, I'd have become mayor sooner. He walks back and forth with that device, sure that in his childhood he imagined that this was to be someone important, but it's no different from the others that call me to do their dirty work. The difference between my pistol and this suit is in the trigger, compared to him, I work with very few bullets."

Mayor Jones leaving the balcony and coming into the room ready for business: — Ah... I'm glad we found you.

Charlie: — You crashed my party.

— Don't worry... You'll have plenty of time to celebrate.

— What do you want?

Then the mayor put whiskey in the glass under the coffee table in front of Charlie: — I want to do business with you.

— You know I'm not a politician's doormat, right? If you're looking for someone to be part of your little games... Get another guy...

— That's why we need you. I'm looking for someone with your skills and your critical sense, you can't ask that of the bag-pushers in my office. Much less the cops, they love blackmail, I'll have to wet their hands monthly, and that sucks... The contact who gave me your name said you're reliable and discreet. I need people like that to do this job... people who know how to be discreet.

Charlie thought again. "What is this guy talking about? Does he think that with this he's going to convince me that I'm a good person? I forgot he's a pro at this. Each one with his own skills, but he's right, there's a lot of guys out there who are just waiting for a politician to make a move on extortion. He needed someone who knows how to work in secret and a little anti-corp idealism... Shit, this guy's good. I think you got the right guy. I think I even know who gave him my contact information."

Charlie: — Tell me... What's going on? Is it with some corporation?

— I think I like you. Straight to the point. Are you willing to go into one of the big ones? One of those... ...that's gonna make you retire?

— I got it. Retirement... The fucked up kind... Cash or graveyard... You know this kind of work can't be trusted, right? There's always someone left... And I'm not the type to let it go cheap.

Jones: — No one is here to fuck with anyone... Don't worry. The parade is peaceful.

Charlie: — Okay. I'll listen to you first and then I'll decide. What do you have for me?

Then the mayor stood up, whiskey glass in hand, took a sip and looked across at Charlie: — The job is with WeaponTech. You got this?

— Holy shit. WeaponTech?

Then the mayor walked over to the window, his back to Charlie: — They're doing some shit in my city hall. One of our hackers found a lot of patches on our network. All indicating a single path... WeaponTech... I wish you could find out what they want with my office. The election's coming up and we have to be careful with everything now.

— You want me to steal their data?

Mayor Jones turned and sat quietly on the couch: — First I

want you to get inside their servers.... Not only do I want to know what they want with my office.... But also...

Charlie felt there was something more... About to be revealed:
— What?

Jones: — Charlie... We've been in proxy infowarfare for a while now. I think the last attack they tried to kill my people, it was their own thing. I've been getting some information from an inside contact on the inside, reliable information, hot stuff, from an engineering guy... He can't go any further, they're already monitoring him up to his neck in there... I lost contact with him a while ago. He's the one who started the speculation. I also found out something about a policeman who opened his mouth in one of these rounds thinking that his partner was trustworthy and ended up revealing that he participated in an outsourced scheme to burn someone from my office. But we are not sure if this information is totally true, it could just be a trap to try something and fuck us. I also want you to find out what they want from us.

Charlie: — Fuck. You can't trust anyone in this fucking city.

Jones: — That's the game... Get used to it... Welcome to politics.

Charlie took a strong sip of his whiskey: — All right... I think I can handle it... But I'm gonna need some help with some resources there.

— All right... But get your people together. I'm gonna give you the seed money to buy what you need for this job, then I'm gonna give you a big fat one. You and your people can drink and talk the shit you always talk every day at NeonDyne.

— What do you mean?

— I'm the mayor. Have you forgotten? I got ears everywhere in town, I know everybody's dirt. You guys fuck up, but I can't forget that you also vote, you also convince who's the most honest guy in town.

— Okay... How much is it?

Mayor Jones pulled a card from his jacket pocket, put it on the table, dragged it toward Charlie, and then tapped it twice with his index finger:-This one here...

Then Charlie looked at the paper, and saw that that amount could retire him and his entire team, even with split amounts: — Fuck... All that Neurocoin? I can't believe it.

— You got a little something there. You merged a corporation with city hall, it's a confidential matter. You gotta move fast. What I can tell you is that this money is real. I'm gonna wire you some extra cash now so you can buy the equipment you need. I already bought some guys who won't notice a big volume of black market gun purchases around town. The police won't get in your way with that. But you're gonna be on your own after that. You can't hold too many guys, the police are decentralized in this city, and many corporations have them in hand.

— I got it. With that much at stake, I'll manage. - Charlie's eyes sparkled: - I'm getting Neurocoin now.

Jones: — There's one more thing. She's coming... New blood in the service around here... But with a lot of skill...

— Damn, new blood? I don't work with rookies.

— You're not a rookie... She's a first line hacker.

Charlie: — First line? Around here?

— Then be careful. I want her in one piece when this job's over... She's a good one.

Then Charlie looked back seeing the door open and there she was entering the room... With leather pants, chrome prosthesis of horizontal facial scratches, robotic vertical scratches by the arms, white colortech in the hair, purple painted nails, leather neckline, looking like she was coming from a sadomasochism store. With purple led sunglasses on the frame and white sneakers with pink led around the soles, while the mayor's security guard at the door said on the sign to another security guard: — Ok. She's here.

Jones: — Ah. So you've arrived.

Without saying anything, coming from behind, she sat on the sofa on Charlie's right side, put her feet up on the coffee table, lit her cigarette with a lighter: — So. Is that the guy who's going to do the job with me?

Jones: — Charlie. Meet the best... Lucy.

Charlie looked over and saw that smoke coming out of her mouth... Like she was used to doing heavy work for the government.

Jones: — She'll break into anything. Whatever you need... She's in... Here's how it's gonna work. You get there and she gets into the system... Simple.

Charlie: — So it's going to be a reconnaissance job... We'll cover her so she can break in and then find out what WeaponTech wants.

Jones: — That's the thing... You guys could start when?

Charlie: — Tomorrow we can start working out a way to get in there... In two days we can get in there.

Jones: — Beauty... I knew I could count on you Charlie... Get your people together and let them know there's Neurocoin waiting for you here... I need this job done as soon as possible. before they make another move against my office.

Charlie: — Don't worry... We'll manage... We'll be quick.

Jones: — Good to know... I don't know... I have a feeling they could act at any moment... It's a weird feeling, I don't know.

Lucy stood up and spoke: — Don't worry... It's going to be okay, Jones.

Charlie: — Beauty... Let's go.

Lucy standing up threw the Driverdata system at Charlie still seated: — You drive.

Charlie took the Driverdata, got up and was ready to leave: — Come on, let's go. I'll let you know soon Jones.

As the two left the room, Jones could be seen looking out the window, glass of whiskey in hand, at the nightscape of Tech City... The swing of his right hand in a circular manner on the glass said that something was going to happen... He didn't know what it was... An uncalculated inaccuracy in his design for government.

Charlie and Lucy chatted on the way to the car, passing through the empty corridors of the building to the elevator. To see if they were in line with their plans.

Charlie: — Yeah... Jones is fucked up... Thinking it was a bed of roses until he gets to City Hall and realizes too late that the city is swallowing him up.

Lucy: — It is the same thing as always with these guys. Trying to preserve their image, I did my last job for him, it was something similar and in the end it was kind of a lie, the focus was just to preserve the image of good samaritan that he built.

Charlie: — I wonder what WeaponTech wants with him.

Lucy: — Probably it is a fight between parties, the opposition must have closed with them to become politically stronger. This is the backstage that nobody talks about, nobody wants to see, the real war, a proxy infwar going on behind the scenes. In the end citizens are just manipulated about who they should vote for. Nobody becomes mayor or councilman around here if there is not a partnership with good corporation behind, but if one fails the other falls together.

Charlie: — Are you telling me that the government goes along with corporations in a proxy infwar under the table to get elected?

Lucy: — Each one chooses one to represent him underneath the curtains. But when things get tough, they call people like us... So that there is no direct conflict between one corporation and another... Here you literally have a warm back, you have a whole technological apparatus protecting you from behind... Fake bots profiles on social networks to influence opinion, buying bloggers and newspaper columnists to manipulate public opinion, fakenews gangs to raise doubts and create a zone of untruths, false reports to ruin someone's image, police investigating to find some dirt and drop everything on the LeakWeb, mass calls of false threats to residents of a place to feel cornered by a party and thus hate it.

As they walked, one could hear the echoes of footsteps in a silent garage.... She kept talking: — That's aside from discounts on enhancements for being affiliated with a certain political party. In some hospitals you are seen first if you are a member of a certain party, some prostheses are almost exclusive to certain loyalists of certain political parties. It is basically a partisan techno-ideological war, mixed with ideological mechanical consumption. When you attack a politician, you are attacking a big company from behind, and when you attack a big company, you are attacking a politician from behind. It is all interconnected.

Charlie in his optics noticed something flashing on the Roadsignal approaching, it was Lucy's vehicle: — Is this it here?

It was that black car with horizontal stripes of red led from one end to the other at the rear, followed by a slightly pointy and rugged front underneath.... Dark chrome detailing around the windows in dark smoked glass. Wide chrome wheels in star shape, white headlights with xenon stripe underneath, black leather seats, black piano details on the doors and dashboard, containing small purple leds with dim lighting inside the black piano, reinforced electromechanical computer central panel with its yellow lap, black screen background and purple letters.

Lucy got in the car, opened the driver's door and said: — Let's go.

The car started, the engine rumbled. It was the now talking... It was time for service.

ONLY ONE OUT

Charlie was driving that nervous night, the two of them going to meet up with the team to start planning the invasion of WeaponTech. Meanwhile... The radio dictated the mood of Tech City in its routine dynamics...

Radio. "Hello Tech City... Another night with stories to tell... This afternoon there was an explosion at the DealDrink bar, four dead and seven injured... When something like this happens, we already know, don't we? We're back to the DeadReeper turf fights between the gangs in Eastcode... But the gossip that's circulating the streets is saying it goes beyond that... They say it could be TigerDream retaliation for the death of Adam, the founder of DrugLink. Adam was true to his roots. He never forgot where he came from, letting everyone know he was funding TigerDream. Until four days ago, near the exit of his company, he was surprised in the car, everyone saw that horror, the motorcycle following the car by the side and shooting against the glass... Unfortunately we ended up losing a great visionary of the TechnoPharmaceutical world... But, as it seems, this power struggle is not going to end well for anyone... Just like last week. Do you remember? The daylight shootout between the NeutronSystems and NanoInviders, exchanging gunfire all the way to the entrance of the Loadyng mall. Where the police were able to take advantage of the breach, closing in and ending the party right there.... Everyone was witness to a shooting show eating loose behind the gangs and witnessed the hunt that ended in over twenty dead."

Charlie went through the street with those purple tunnel ceiling lights and the yellow side, coming out of there, turned on the blinker to the right, just another course of some sort, just past the bridge he was home... Near NeonDyne... Without stopping paying attention, they kept listening to the news of the day on the radio...

Radio. "But, let's talk about good things... InsideLife has just implemented their new system on Texture. Now users will be able to use the subreality without any more time worries. Their new system will slow down the synaptic acceleration of some perceptual points in order to accelerate the conditioning within Texture... Users will be able to enjoy the new reality in a much more scaled time, separate from the time of reality. InsideLife believes that this new technology will be able to bring more life to Texture with a longer dwelling time, where its users will be able to enjoy it without fear of getting lost in time in their lives. We can't forget that many people have a changed life, they left everything of reality to have a life inside Texture's subreality. I'm not here to judge anyone. What matters is to feel good, wherever you are... But InsideLife is already ahead of schedule before they start thinking about changes in the prison system. The sentence time will be the same in the real body of the prisoners, there will be no change in the rehabilitation process in Texture made exclusively for the prisoners to be able to return to society... Human rights and activists are against this form of work that exploits the minds of the inmates, living as vegetables, making many prefer to die than go to the Tech City prison and serve as vegetables for some corporation... InsideLife refuted all accusations, saying that now they will have a more rehabilitative job and can guarantee a better future... The guys can live and work all day in sub-reality. In return they leave Texture believing in a renewed life, feeling healed. Of course, companies also gain from this, good old supply and demand; after all, nothing is free in this city. "

As the news circulated on the radio, Charlie looked ahead, driving and focused on the street while talking to Lucy: — I've never found you doing any work around here. A first line hacker around here would be well known around here by now.

Lucy: — I used to work with the Slim Nets, I was a Hook, responsible for mapping cyber-attacks against our gang... I also hacked into the shadow systems to erase the traces on Cybernet.

Charlie: — But... How did you end up here? It's not exactly like leaving the Slim Nets... It's a pretty crazy crowd, the kind you get in and you don't get out.

Lucy: — One thing led to another, you know. After they took down NoobShark, we were never able to get back together. Sometimes a few manage to communicate, but he was the central source that brought us the good stuff. Now it's every man for himself. We're taking anything that comes our way. Now things are a lot more dangerous and it's gonna get worse. Imagine a city where the top guys are out there working on the side.

Charlie: — Fuck... You actually did jobs with NoobShark? The Tech City legend? Now I get it... That's why you got to the big time. With me it was almost the same thing.

Crossing that bridge with electronic signs, the sides full of neon and the background of large buildings, were nervous to start planning the scheme to steal the data from WeaponTech. Then in the crossroad in the exit of the viaduct two cars crossed in front and one arrived hitting from behind, it was a frenetic bid that was about to roll ... Then Charlie shouted: — *Get the fuck down!*

They began to shoot, they were machine gun bursts against the car from the front and from behind, you could clearly see that someone didn't just want to finish the job, but also to leave a message. It was when Lucy spoke: — Fuck. They are fucking shooting at us.

She watched crouched in her seat as bullets whizzed across the car, none hitting Charlie crouched in the steering wheel, who swerved to the side ready to throw the car off the bridge. As the bullet ate away at the steel, he accelerated all the way to the side causing the car to fall off the top of the bridge, the car sped down into the water, ready to slam on its beak and do some damage. It was when Lucy heard Charlie's scream: — HOLD *ON... FUCK!!!!*

As the water was releasing from the impact, the headlights silhouetted the tracer bullets fired from above the bridge. The car was sinking and the bullets were going through the roof. Making the two of them quickly get out of the car and they could see those bullets scraping the chrome steels of their bodies, plunging deep into that Tech City rot. That's when she turned on the LightV and saw everything cleaner under the water like a filter able to see behind the river's dirt... And through her eyes she saw a spill of light water underneath the avenue below the overpass exit... As the bullets passed between them, she beckoned Charlie to follow her. He could only see lapses of her feet traversing in lines over the water until they entered the sewer exit.

And so they saw that from up there began to increase the number of shooters. A helicopter started to fly over with light where the car had fallen. Several police cars closing the bridge, those blue and red lights were multiplying from up there. As they looked down on that madness that started out of nowhere.

Then he said: — What the fuck is going on?

Lucy: — Someone tipped off the scam.   Some son of a bitch threw WeaponTech our way.

Charlie: — It's not like that... The scheme doesn't work like that... What the fuck, what the fuck... Everything was ready to get us. Damn, that mayor son of a bitch betrayed us.

Lucy: — It may not have been him... Jones wouldn't gain anything with us dead. There's something different about this... It's not good shit.

Charlie: — That's him, all right. The government teamed up with corporations to take our kind one by one. They hunt people like us. We must be on their blacklist... They were trying to get me.

Lucy: — You don't think he would set up a whole scheme just to get us, do you? Let go of this paranoia. Let's try to be rational.

Charlie: — Look at that shit up there. You're gonna tell me I'm wrong... You're gonna say that's paranoid up there... They act together... I don't know why I didn't see it before. They're out to get me. They teamed up with Nakamura. I knew they wouldn't let it go cheap.

Lucy: — If he wanted to, he would have killed you already. Me too.

Charlie: — Wake the fuck up. That's not how it works. They fake a robbery and catch the guy on the sly.

Lucy: — I know. A robbery with those bullets all over us, no one would believe it.

Charlie: — Come on Lucy. Get real. This is Tech City. Nobody gives a shit. One more body, one less body. Whatever the newspapers say is good to keep the lie that everybody wants to tell, nobody wants to get involved in the death of people like us.

Lucy: — Let's get out of here...

Charlie: — I think there might be a path through here. It could lead into the city. Maybe we can get to NeonDyne.

On the way to NeonDyne they saw the police cars circulating everywhere, beating up junkies, aggressively approaching people on the street... A guy from a gang got scared and ran out, shooting back without looking and was killed right there, shot in the back, his body on the asphalt left aside... The goal of that night wasn't to gather bodies, was to leave bodies, find the targets and make an example of them. Helicopters circulated and caught by surprise the people with the lights pointed on the alleys. Nobody remembers much of seeing a hunt like that around the city, everybody seemed uncontrolled for the first time, it was almost a war atmosphere that could be about to burst, an internal war due the massive abuse of the authorities... The order was, in the doubt, to arrive shooting... But it wasn't like that; the gangs wouldn't let anything go cheap.

***

Arriving at NeonDyne Charlie and Lucy went to the guys table, that's when Jeniffer with purple hair tied up, vertical prosthesis of exposed scratches on her thighs over pink leather pants, tight white blouse and black leather jacket... Sitting back in her chair, finishing her drink she said: - Haven't you heard?

— They killed Jones... The mayor. — Spoke Alex balding with an earring in his left ear, white tank top, strong and a little thin... Sitting on the leather bench with his feet on the seat holding a bottle of booze.

Charlie: — Fuck. How did he die? How did you guys find out?

— It's all over the news. - Said Ryan wearing black tank top, strong, horizontal denture line on his face and a square red lens in front of his right eye. His right arm was chrome prosthesis, in it containing the tattoo of a military bulldog in beret, smiling cigarette in the mouth with teeth well exposed and holding a machine gun.

Jeniffer: — Who's that?

Charlie: — This is Lucy. She's reliable... She's with us... Relax.

Lucy: — Do you know who did it?

Alex: — Not yet. No suspects.

That's when Lucy and Charlie looked at each other; they knew it was a file burn. They were being hunted and nobody but them knew anything about anything. It was when Charlie decided to open the game with the team: — Guys. Remember that guy who came here? He was Jones' security guard. I just talked to him a little while ago.

Ryan: — Damn man. Are they blaming you guys for his death?

Lucy: — We don't know. What we do know is that my car was shot to the last. It turned into paper.

Jeniffer: — Then you guys are fucked. You might be thinking it was you.

Lucy: — Just like they called Charlie, they also called me for the same job... All I had to do was arrive and take care of the money.

Charlie: — I think it has something to do with WeaponTech.

Jeniffer: — Fuck. Is WeaponTech involved?

Lucy: — The field was for them.

Jeniffer: — And you went along with this, Charlie? Didn't you think about what you were getting involved in? WeaponTech equips the military with state-of-the-art combat systems... I've been wanting to take these motherfuckers down for a long time. But even I know they're fucked up, you can't just walk in there.

Ryan: — What's the deal with them?

Charlie: — Stealing data. It was a proxy infowar between WeaponTech and Mayor Jones' office. They were trying to fuck up his candidacy.

Lucy: — I think we should go after them. Whatever tipped these guys off to the point where they killed Jones. It's something that should be worth a lot in the marketplace. And another thing... If they're hunting us... They're gonna find you soon enough and they'll hunt you down, too.

Charlie: — We're fucked. We won't make it out of the city. They're gonna chase us to the end of the world. The only way is to get into WeaponTech and see what was behind all this shit involving Jones' office. Maybe then we can get a bargain, a way out.

Jeniffer: — It won't be long before they get to us and it's on us.

Ryan: — There is no other way out.

Charlie: — Before we left, he left some money with me to get some irons and apparatus to invade.

Lucy: — For me he also left...

Jeniffer: — Beauty. I already have an idea. It's going to be full of guards there.

Charlie: — I think I know what you're getting at... We impersonate WeaponTech security...

Jeniffer: — We know a guy who has some unique cloths and apparatus that can camouflage from the DiskJet ID, and so we can bypass the whole system.

Lucy: — DiskJet is temporary. It won't bypass it completely... Their scheme does break the BloodProxy and over time identifies the real nature of the blood of the person who is there... It's a system they implemented after they broke their security of facial capture and artificial intelligence all three ways.

Jeniffer stared... And Charlie interrupted: — She's a first line hacker.

The others looked at each other and began to see Lucy with new eyes. What was a first line hacker doing there? Now they were frightened by her presence that explained all her technological wisdom to the cave people.

Lucy: — These guys can be paranoid about security... But I am more... I developed a paradoxical compound from Metalink that makes their artificial intelligence circulate and find a fake profile in the system, and after two minutes it changes the profile. It takes three minutes of fake profile in the paradox compound to set off the alarms. And also if she keeps looking for too long will turn on the alarm.

Ryan: — How do we get in and out of there?

Lucy: — We go in with parachutes coated with synthetic alloy of titanium powders with a polarized graphene, so it is not identified by the anti-aircraft artillery. Their system identifies the high elevation of the fabric and plastic for the assumption of parachutes... Well, helicopters flying directly overhead, no way.

Jeniffer: — How do we get out of there?

Charlie: — We can jump off the building... And fall near the river... We leave a boat in the river and from there we disappear. River security is weak... and the guys have a river right near there. All we're gonna have to do is deactivate the water mines in that area.

Lucy: — I have an anti-ballistic magnet that can help. These mines are composed of magnets that go into defragmentation process to the touch, is an intelligent system of water mines... But with this system I developed, we can touch them that nothing will happen, they absorb the impact, and identify as force water, water objects, fish and even another mine touching ... We're not going to have a problem with that.

Jeniffer: — How are we going to find their core system?

Lucy: — You can leave it to me. I know where it is... I talked to Jones before Charlie got to the building... He gave me the right way to get there. He got his hands wet with a guy who had the building's blueprint and the location of the sectors... It's all in my biodisk.

Ryan: — Come on then... Let's go get these guys.

Jeniffer: — Let me get the irons ready, we'll burn whatever comes our way.

Alex: — I can get the boat for us.

Charlie: — We can't do everything today. We have to hold on for tomorrow.

Lucy: — It could be twenty-four hours before they realize that you have a connection with us... It could take time.

Jeniffer: — That'll give us time to get ready... We'll start getting the schematics tonight.

Mia with the silver samurai sword propped up beside her, dressed in black clothes, green hair and chrome prosthesis on her left arm, smoking with her legs propped up above the table: — And what are we waiting for? Let's throw these motherfuckers in then. I wanted to burn some more steel today... See some circuits on fire...

After a while of planning the guys were leaving the table to do their part and set up everything to invade WeaponTech... Lucy held Charlie's arm and said: — Charlie. I have to talk to you alone.

He saw that different look... He didn't know what it was... Still in doubt of something hidden in the hacker's memorial mechanical depths: — Okay. Let's sit here.

Then he told his team: — We're coming — And everyone confirmed... And they were getting ready, leaving through the back of NeonDyne. Then Charlie and Lucy sat down and followed taking the rest of the drink that had in their glasses.

Lucy: — You know Charlie... This is all new to me. I don't know... After NoobShark was taken down, everything changed... We split up, we each got our own freelance jobs. But the truth is I don't really know where I am.

Charlie: — You lost the guy who kept you in line.

Lucy: — I worked with a team, it was almost all killed... NoobShark was not only the leader of the Slim Nets... Not only was he the guy who kept me in line... In fact... he was my father.

Charlie: — Fuck... You are the daughter of the Tech City legend.

Lucy: — He got along with Jones. That's why I could get a job with him... He helped me in the beginning with some jobs... But then I started to get along, and in the end I was working together with Jones... We got along great. Fuckin' hell.

Lucy began to cry lightly, trying to hold back her tears: — I can't believe it. Everybody's going through this shit... It's all fucked up... There's only me left, man.

Charlie: — Don't worry. You're with us now. The guys are a little crazy, but they're good people...

Lucy: — It all started to fall apart. Sometimes I wonder. Could it be that they are not after me? Destroying everything I know?

Charlie: — What do you mean Lucy?

Lucy: — Out of nowhere things started happening. What if they... Really existed? What do they want from me? Where are they? They seem to act in the form of events and accidents... Like they know something about me.

Charlie: — I don't understand the direction of our conversation.

Lucy: — Neither do I. It feels like something is chasing me. It's not an energy. I don't know what it is. Or it could just be my paranoia. I have dreamed a few times when I was running in a street and everything was falling apart behind me... I was running, but it seemed like this thing that was making everything fall apart was coming closer... It feels like it's a conscience chasing me.

Charlie: — Is it not the lack of a maternal presence?

Lucy: — Could be. NoobShark said that my mother died when I was very young. I don't remember exactly what happened to her... I never knew what it was like to live with a mother figure... It was because of her death that he turned into the hacker he was.

Charlie: — I understand. But you are not alone. You can have your own family. We're here. All of us on the team are alone... Bunch of fucking loners... Lost in Tech City, each with a story worse than the other. I think you'll fit in with us.

Lucy: — Thank you Charlie. We just met. I shouldn't open up to you like this... but... I don't know what to say to you...

Charlie: — It's okay Lucy... I know what it's like to be desperate...

Lucy then smiled slightly at Charlie, her eyes sparkling neon pink: — Thank you.

He touched his hands, the steels touched each other, a transcendentalized mechanical connection, where behind every cybernetic body had something still human, a feeling of mercy, a feeling that only humans are able to feel, that feeling of shelter, having as a symbol of this feeling completed with Charlie's words: — You are with us now.

WHERE HAVE WE BEEN

Descending through the modified parachutes, they reached the top, the top of the madcap waiting with an entire WeaponTech army... Little circular chips stuck to the antiaircraft guns, while those red dots flashed... From high up in the parachutes Lucy's eyes glowed.... The guns turned off... Everyone heard her on the radio, *"Okay... I've broken in."* A sphere that fell on the top floor molded itself and stuck like glue.... Her eyes glowed again *"I knocked out the presence sensors and weight identifiers"*. Another chip hit two cameras that flashed on the security screens that transmitted the same thing as minutes ago.... When they arrived they were collecting their parachutes just as Lucy walked over to the camera where she plugged the wire on top of her wrist and spoke: - I redid the image transmission on the cameras... These here gave me access to all the others... Now no one else can identify us. I used this access to penetrate the Metalink paradox in the three-way ID of the motion system so we could move around inside with fake profiles without weirding out their artificial intelligence. I think we'll be fine.

Now that's what you call a first line hacker... Jeniffer deferred impressed looks to Charlie and felt the power on the spot when she saw Lucy easily hacking into systems with state-of-the-art military cryptography... Lucy didn't warn... She arrived putting her pussy on the table and showing why she had come to this mission... Jeniffer realized and came to her senses... that they wouldn't be able to get close to WeaponTech if it weren't for Lucy's skills.

Starting to enter the building you could see those triggers ready and dashing in ready for the clash... Ryan talking: — Yeah, fuck... Let's hit these motherfuckers... Fuck with these WeaponTech assholes.

Lucy in the front with Charlie coming down the stairs: — Here... Come down this way... I'm passing the Myndmap to you. You see the signal on your neurograph? It's four floors down... Near the open area of the building... Where you can see all the floors.

Coming a little far from the room... She was on the other side of the same floor... But the problem was that that technology had no connection with WeaponTech, as if it was something separate from the building... Even the colors on the walls. The employees walking... Some with white overalls that covered the whole body... Lucy realized at the time that the thing was different... She plugged her wrist into the first door and spoke: - Damn it. I think it's gonna be fucked up.

Charlie: — What do you mean Lucy?

Lucy: — This one is different... It is an intelligent system coupled in a cryptographic that performs semantic reading in the transformation of the keys... I found here another bridge...

Jeniffer: — What?

Lucy: — I can open the doors... But it will set off the alarms... It'll be a silent alarm... A fucking alarm.

Charlie: — Shit.

Mia: — Fuck you Lucy... There's no going back anyway.

Lucy: _ I opened... But get ready because the alarm went off

Ryan: — Fuck... First one to breathe is going to take a few bursts.

When he just opened the door of the room... The first to enter was Alex, who fired the machine gun at the first employee he saw, were bursts in that white coat all perforated of blood by the bullets... The machine gun attacked at all: — Fuck. I got scared... This crazy appeared out of nowhere in front of me. Now it's over... Fuck me.

Jeniffer Quietly threw a P.E. M sphere down below the building, into the open system between the floors... Soon it slowed down some auxiliary security systems, shutting down some weapons... rendering them unusable. Conflict cyborgs went down and shut down with the protoshock. But out of nowhere the alarm started ringing something, the floors turned red Charlie then said: — That's it, guys. Our trademark, come out and play the whorehouse.

They came in crazy, machine gunning people, no matter if it was security or not... They were caught off guard. If you moved, you were the enemy, the only thing you had in mind... That's when several military men came in, armed to the teeth... Firing as they climbed the stairs to the open part of the building. The team was forced to take cover on the pillars above to dodge the RPGs. while others were going to the floors above. Some drones went up. Noticing that, Lucy launched a cybernetic grenade, programmed to attack similar ones. A lightning shot hit the drones that started to shoot themselves and the military that were going up the stairs... Carrying out suicide attacks throwing itself until down there, exploding close to the guards.

Even with Lucy's invasion attempt, the door was left a little between open... Mia already used the prosthesis to open the other closed door: — We are coming.

When they saw that pile of shimmering glass they didn't understand anything, the Cybermind logo stamped on that glass structure around electric goo, electric rays were shooting around that goo protected by those glasses separated from each other, a circle of several glasses around... Having information passing inside them, words, images and sometimes even the low sounds of conversations... And the team knew at once that there was a different parade never seen before. Lucy understood more or less what was going on and went straight to a room where there were four engineers: — Damn. What is happening here?

Startled, engineer Dylan spoke up: — It doesn't touch anything. Here we connect directly to Neurodatta.

Charlie: — What the fuck? Neurodatta? What the fuck is that?

Engineer Isabelle quickly interrupted: — What occurs here is Neurodatification... A nuclear pole of Neurodatta's technosocial system...

Jeniffer: — I don't understand anything... What do you mean man? What is this?

Lucy: — This is where Jones wanted us to go... Charlie... This was it.

The engineer Joshua then answered Lucy: — Jones? You're talking about that backstabbing son of a bitch.

Lucy then put the pistol to the engineer's temple and said: — Don't talk about Jones, you son of a bitch. Surely he was worth more than you.

Ryan excited about Lucy's willingness to kill... He did: — Pull that trigger, man. Put that motherfucker out.

Charlie held the barrel of the gun down: — Easy there Lucy. Let's see what he's got for us — He pointed to the core- What's that, man?

Joshua: — Don't you see? It's information.

Mia then shouted from the door — They're coming. Alex: — Speak the fuck up... What the fuck is this? Isabelle: — It's information...

Lucy: — Don't tell me that's what I'm thinking?

Dylan: — It's information from the entire city.

Charlie: — Fuck... Information from what? From the cameras? From virtual accesses?

Dylan: — No man... You're innocent anyway. It's people's thoughts... The thoughts of all of Tech City.

Charlie: — Fuck... What does WeaponTech do with some shit like that?

Lucy dropped the weapons, sat down on the chair, put her hands on her head: — My God... This can't be happening... This is not real... It can't be... I must be dreaming.

Charlie: — What's going on Lucy?

Lucy disconsolate: — I don't believe it... It's a lie... So everything was true.

Ryan: — Hey... Next... We'll take the guys with us... WeaponTech can make a trade...

Jeniffer: — Alex... Press them... We're taking them with us.

Suddenly they saw Mia taking pistol shots and then suffering bursts of gunfire from her body in the doorway of the room... Being shot by a heavily armed squad... The noise was deafening and the bullets going through her body hit the wall and the Neurodatta's windows... And as soon as they entered the room they were met with bullets... That frantic gunfire exchange rolling loose with Mia's body on the floor having stares over a pool of blood, riddled with short circuits... The glass breaking and the bullet eating... The squad propped up on the walls, tables and small walls. When Alex appeared over a wall to hit a guy in the face and was met with a bullet in the forehead, falling straight to the ground... After that... The squad machine gunned one of the four engineers mercilessly when he stood up and asked them to stop because he wanted to go with them... Flying backwards and his coat being pierced by bullets splashing blood on Charlie's team. He died simply by standing in their way. As Dylan jumped through the glass that led to the other side of the room, falling to the floor below. Isabelle and Joshua managed to run down the side of the wall towards the squad as one of the squad guys called out to them from the corner.

Jeniffer ran to the other side of the room, which made a glass corridor saying *"This way"*... It was when they hit her belly, being surprised by another squad coming from the other side... Just waiting on the lookout... Backing up she looked forward, seeing directly to those gun barrels prepared in a hidden way in the darkness of the end of the corridor... Soon the fires and sparks danced to the sound of the shots... ...Shooting his body... You could see the pieces of flesh, remains of implants, irons everywhere, mixed with blood gushing into the room... It was Jeniffer being shot from the front... Even though she fell... The guys didn't forgive, they kept shooting her on the floor to confirm that nothing there would ever stand up again.

Then Ryan became enraged getting up from behind the wall where he was protecting himself.... Charlie screamed: — *Ryan... No!!!*

Ryan ran out into the hallway where Jeniffer was shot... machine gunning the guys who couldn't take the heavy calibers tearing their bodies apart... Falling to the floor like paper. They'd never seen a crazy motherfucker like that in their life... Killing the guys, bullets passing close to his body and not giving a damn about his own life ... Then, the guards coming from behind those who were being shot, ended up shooting and hitting him... He entered in a game in which he ended up being shot and shooting at the same time the guys in an exchange of death... Realizing he was powerless to continue... he went for it all or nothing. Pulled out two grenades, holding one in each hand and threw himself along with them to the guards: — YOU *WANT A GOOD FUCKING? THEN YOU WILL SEE WHAT IT IS TO FUCK FOR REAL... YOU SONS OF BITCHES!!!*

Causing a tremendous explosion on the way out of the room through the back corridor... starting a huge short circuit in the glass information system... Charlie and Lucy propped up behind the wall with nowhere to go. There was silence. Only the fire of the corridor burning loose, the smoke coming out of the machine gun barrels and the sound of the bullets bouncing on the floor.

Right up until the moment one of the security guards yelled:
— Okay... The joke's over... It's about time you guys turned yourselves in... And maybe we'll let one of you live...

The way on the other side was closed... In that front corridor there was only the entire squadron of nervous finger. And below the information system and nuclear dissipator connected under the goo with electric beams... There was no way out... So Charlie and Lucy got up with P.E. M, as a last resort to threaten to throw him into the central information hub... And as they made a false surrender motion. A startled soldier fired first, the rest went along to make sure, making Charlie and Lucy suffer bursts of gunfire. Under the fright of the shots hitting their bodies, they fell in the electrified goo... Dropping the P.E.M., causing even more damage to the floor and the goo. The opposite happened, instead of shutting down the electrical structures, they ended up shorting out the room.

Through the goo... They both fell to the floor below... Starting small explosions upstairs... Followed by large short bursts that began to drive the guards away... until it caused explosions to cascade throughout the entire floor. From far away it was there... The WeaponTech building with that floor on fire as the fumes rose... Leaving a doubtful observation in who watched the flames from down there... about what had happened in one of Tech City's most secure buildings.

WAKE OF TOMORROW

Charlie waking up in bed seeing from behind that medical chair, dentist chair style, only seeing one arm out... That guy on top of it, going through the body's electronics, wearing a mask and wearing a lab coat covered in blood, saying: — Don't fucking die... You can do it... Stay with me.

That electric pulse in the chest, gushing blood. It looked like the room of a small apartment, the back of the doctor there was a mirror on the wall, looking like a place to put on makeup, but what he had there was not makeup, but gears, prostheses and loose electronics. Charlie went back to sleep, not understanding anything that was happening... When he woke up again... His eyes dazzled what looked like a small room with a bed next to the other, beep noise at the side monitoring his heartbeat... He looked to the side and saw Lucy unconscious, soon he realized that the electronic door opened and he was coming in.... Dylan with blood on his lab coat, without the mask talking: — Fuck. You almost went from this to better.

Charlie: — What happened.

Dylan: — Get some sleep Charlie. We have a lot to talk about... But first, you need to get some rest.

A while later Charlie and Lucy woke up practically together, feeling pain in their chests. Some bullet wounds still hurt a little, it was still a little hard to get up... Then one sat facing the other... And without saying a word the silence brought all the words needed to expose their looks... They were alive... That was what mattered.

That's when Dylan walked in: — You're awake. I'm glad you're getting better.

Charlie: — What the fuck happened man? What did you do?

Lucy: — Why did you help us? We were supposed to be scrap metal now.

Dylan: — You guys better calm down.

Lucy: — What? I don't like that look.

Understanding both of their doubts, Dylan quickly grabbed a chair and approached them to talk: — I saved your lives... I managed to catch you both when you fell down there when the explosions started.

Charlie: — Why did you do that? You're with them, man.

Dylan: — That's where you're wrong. No one said anything about me?

Charlie got an expression of not understanding anything... But Dylan noticed that it was obvious that he didn't know his identity and soon continued talking: — Oh, good... Good that nobody knows anything about me.

Lucy: — What are you talking about?

Dylan: — I was working with Jones... I was the guy who had been passing the information to him.

Charlie: — He told me he had an engineer from inside WeaponTech... But I never would have guessed it was you. You were with them developing that thing?

Dylan looked a little sad: — Yes. I was, but by the time I realized what we were doing it was too late. There was no going back... There's no way you could get rid of something like that. You know?

Lucy: — After all. What was that there?

Charlie: — Were they really people's thoughts?

Dylan: —Yeah. They were.

Charlie: — You're such a son of a bitch. Taking away everybody's privacy... What a crazy thing to read the thoughts of all those people.

Dylan: — I think it was a prototype... still in testing.   Lucy: — And what is yours with Jones.

Dylan: — I was helping him expose the scam... Something like that in the wrong hands would be a hell of a problem. Imagine an ill-intentioned politician knowing what people are thinking?

Charlie: — You helped them do that shit... Don't get yours out of the way... You're part of the problem too... You helped create it there.

Lucy: — And what does this have to do with Jones?

Dylan: — You don't know... Jones was working with WeaponTech under the covers. They're the ones who helped get him elected. But he would never support something like that.

Charlie: — Are you trying to tell me that Jones was working with WeaponTech? And that deep down he might actually be an honest politician in this town?

Dylan: — I'm not saying he was honest. I'm looking for someone honest around here. I'm saying he wouldn't support a project where you could invade people's privacy. Not on that level. That's why in some events he probed some issues with some engineers, suspicious of some projects that could make him put everything at stake... And then we met at an event, we had the same ideas about people's privacy... He was an advocate of decentralized technology, as well as an advocate of free speech combined with privacy. Jones convinced me that what I was doing was wrong, without even knowing the project I was working on. So I went to him soon after. Saying some things that had been happening in a hidden way at WeaponTech.

Lucy: — And what did he do?

Dylan: — That's when things got thicker... They started stalking and planning the deaths of people connected to your office. Thinking the leaked information might be coming from there. They started to pursue and try to kill him... He was always tough, but there was no other way out. I guess you guys were his last resort.

Charlie: — Fuck. Now he's gone. It didn't do any good what we did... Those WeaponTech motherfuckers.

Dylan: — Now you're dead. It's all over the papers. Your entire team has been accused of killing Jones. The word is out that all of you were killed by WeaponTech. So they got carte blanche with the deputy mayor.

Charlie: — Fucking sons of bitches.

Lucy: — I don't believe it. Jones. You didn't tell us anything.

Charlie: — That's why one of the guys said Jones was a traitor.

Dylan: — Yes. Some people already knew about this war.

Lucy: — And who are they?

Dylan: — Who?

Charlie: — The guys who were with you.

Dylan: — You don't want to know. They're the worst kind. They're the brains behind the whole project... They're not WeaponTech employees like me... They're directly connected to Cybermind.

Charlie: — Who are they?

Dylan: — Isabelle and Joshua... They're Cybermind engineers. They built the whole project... And there's an even worse story behind them.

Charlie: — History?

Dylan: — Not many people talked, but I think it was just history. Some of the other engineers that came along with the project... They said they were way beyond that.

Lucy: - What do you mean far beyond? Did they have a cybernetic consciousness built in?

Charlie: — What do you mean Lucy?

Lucy: — Some rumors I've heard around... About Cybermind having a cybernetic consciousness.

Dylan: — No. Much worse... The rumors were that they had developed a cybernetic unconsciousness system that linked directly to people's thoughts.

Charlie: — Fuck. What do you mean man?

Dylan: — They were just rumors. Stories... Urban legends. Those hallway things... But that they could change people's thinking... Change their behavior... Things like that.

Lucy began to cry lightly: — I can't believe... I can't believe... I was right... It was them... Those sons of bitches.

Charlie started looking suspiciously at Lucy: — What happened Lucy?

Lucy: — My dreams... The messages I received... The investigations I made...

Dylan, not understanding Lucy's remarks... He continued: — The rumours were that they had a system that penetrated through the cybernetic field, reaching the outflows, charge fissures and discharges of the nervous system and was able to enter the unconscious and thereby modify it.

Charlie: — Fuck... What if this isn't just a rumor Dylan? What if all this shit is true?

Dylan: — Something should have happened to us by now.

Charlie: — I don't know, man... From everything we've seen... I can't believe this.

Dylan: — I thought about it a lot... But... I'll be right back. I have to get something to show you.

So Dylan left the room... Leaving only Charlie and Lucy in the room... He felt something in the air, like it was the urge to ask something that was going on with Lucy and at the same time Lucy's feeling of revealing some secret hidden behind her woes.

Charlie: — What is it Lucy?

Lucy sad not knowing whether to say everything or not: — I don't know how to explain it to you.

Charlie: — Start with trust... You can trust me to talk about what ails you.

Lucy: — When I was an adult, I used to ask my father about

my mother... He would always fight me saying that she was killed in a gang fight in the streets... I always looked for who the guys were and never found anything... Until one day I saw him talking to a guy at a sign... About a conscience that should be released, where I ended up hearing the voice of the guy on the other side of the line, telling him to forget her... She had already turned into a cybernetic consciousness... That could only carry electrical pulses of sensations of her presence in him, he had nothing else to do, if not this consciousness would pursue him and he would be risking a lot, including the life of his own daughter, if he kept wanting to know more about her whereabouts.

Charlie: — Bloody animals... They kept a person trapped in their system... They're monsters.

Lucy: — I started to feel different things, some strange dreams, I talked about them with my father who said he was also dreaming... He said that this was normal. It was when he told me about a cybernetic legend, where we live in a great unconscious system that molds our short circuits. An absolute consciousness capable of helping our feelings... Almost like a cybernetic entity present in our lives... The binarism that took life and today is part of a great neural net of which we are part in our day by day... Just pieces, small cracks of the unconscious, developing a great collective unconscious, transformed to an absolute consciousness.

Then a tear came out of Lucy's eye, falling a drop on the cold steel of her hand: — When I have certain dreams, I think it's her. She is there, watching me... This great consciousness, trying to give me a caress in the nights of despair... In my moments of loneliness this cybernetic force gives me the impulse to continue to breathe, to feel life... Then I start to feel something different... Something transcendent behind all this steel, behind all these enhancements and components... A spirit helping my way, a cybernetic road composed of lights above every dark abyss... It's not above me, it's not something absolute, it's a feeling from within that connects me with a singularity.... Impossible to describe... It is this energy that is in everything, a perfect electricity.

Charlie: — Maybe it's her. Lucy: - Yeah. Maybe.

Charlie: — She could be with you... Protecting you.

Lucy: — The most bizarre thing. It's that after that day of him talking to this guy. A short time later he died. They murdered him, raiding our place, hunting us down one by one. And I had this feeling that wherever I went, this thing behind my mind was chasing me... It wasn't her... I think it was them. I didn't know who or what it was... Today. Dylan telling me that. I think it's them, Charlie. I think it's the Cybermind. It's after my conscience. What they want with me, I don't know.

Charlie: — They won't catch you Lucy. I won't let them.

Then Charlie looked into Lucy's eyes... His eyes glowed blue sparkling, hers light pink... As they looked at each other, they saw something different, all that steel seemed more chromed, their hearts sped up and their breaths were panting... As soon as they touched each other's hands, they felt for the first time something beyond the touch of the skin through the steel... It was a different touch, it felt like the touch of presence, continuity, that they were no longer alone.

When their lips touched, their tongues entered into a cosmic dance, accompanying the composition of the music of their hearts, where the harmony of the body corresponded with the gasping breaths. One soul, where the zero and the one came together. Destroying all perception of binarism for full singularity. All is known and all is unknown. Every sensation is new, nothing is the same. It is different every second. Interweaving the steels, electrical components and enhancements into a single chromatic dance. The shine of chrome was evident in the euphoria of the touches on the body and face, they wanted to feel more, tear the skin, scratch the steel, know the real nature of what it is to be human. Where the one and the multiple connected under something interconnected and unknown, almost as if it were the essence of the connection, the beauty of being present in the moment, making the immediate speak and the connection scream through the silence of closed eyes... Together... In one energy.

When they opened their eyes... They saw... That everything was perfect.

That's when Dylan came into the room with different components, they were small like the size of a card. His look was worried, his voice was a little fumbled, he didn't know how to say that... give that kind of news: — There's one more thing.

Charlie: — What happened?

Dylan: better listen to me very carefully.

Lucy: — What happened?

Dylan: — When you fell into the electric goo, composed of the nuclear fissure, blasting the P.E.M. into that maelstrom of information... something happened to your bodies.

Lucy and Charlie looked worriedly at Dylan... Nothing would come this easy.

Dylan: — When I was fixing you, I noticed something irreparable, connected to your central nervous system... Some kind of electromagnetic conductor. I put it into the system to pull up the data and check it out... And everything indicated to me something different, I did and re-calculated to find a solution. And I found even more problems. That's when I realized. It wasn't an electromagnetic conductor. You were conducting electromagnetically through your system, it's almost like a time bomb. I didn't understand why, but as your bodies separated, the electromagnetic charge increased. So I went to check, your bodies are connected to a huge pulse. As if it wasn't possible to be separated, but this pulse system is increasing and soon both of you will die.

Charlie: — Holy shit. Are you telling me I'm going to die?

Dylan: — You will feel pain... that pulse will increase.

Lucy: — What the fuck man... What the fuck... Now that...

Dylan: — And it gets even worse... That mixture of the compounds made something that could look like a P.E.M. system interlocked with nuclear reagent that could tear apart all the information... Like a pulse that would shut down all the information around it, like a nuclear bomb. You know that no EMP causes brain damage in our cybernetic bodies. But this nuclear pulse of information is gonna do some serious damage. A lot of people are gonna die.

Charlie: — Holy shit, man. You're telling me that not only are we gonna die. We're gonna kill a bunch of people?

Dylan: — I believe it will be pretty much all of Tech City.

Lucy: — Holy shit. We're fucked... We are fucked.

Dylan: — There's no point in even you killing yourselves. If one of you dies... This shit blows up. No one will see anything explode. Everyone in the city will just shut down for good.

Charlie: — Then we'll be forced to leave town.

Dylan: — You can't even leave the city. The information receiver was linked directly to the Cybermind's central core... Looks like you guys are interconnected to the core... I don't know how you haven't exploded yet... But just as you two can't stay away from each other. You can't stay away from the core either.

Charlie: — Holy shit. There's no way we can survive this.

Dylan: — I've been studying what happened to you since then... I'm looking at a way to reverse the situation. Luckily I managed to steal the polarized conductor that connects to the Cybermind's information core. I have it for a while, I had stolen it when I was at WeaponTech, it seems now that this system is useful. I made some modifications to it, and I was able to create these components that show when you guys are far away from each other. It will beep... While it is green, it means everything is ok, yellow means you are in a medium distance... Red means you're too far apart, and if you get any further apart, it could pop. But the most worrying thing is that over time it may cause you to have to get closer together... There will come a time when you are almost dying and at the same time it will be impossible to stay away from each other.

Lucy: — We have no way out Charlie... We're really screwed.

Dylan: — I believe this is also happening with Cybermind core... See? That green on the left side is the distance one has from the other. The right side is with the Cybermind core, now it's yellow.

Charlie then took his card: — Beauty.

Lucy took the card and said: — So... The only way out is for us to go to Cybermind?

Dylan: — I'm still seeing a way. It might be possible to reverse it. But I think that only you people inside Neurodatta can modify this pulse. It is the data processing circulating at high speed within you that is feeding this pulse. I think if you can transfer that data, you can get rid of... But it's only a hypothesis. The data repels a high spin that is feeding the electromagnetism that is circulating within you.

What happens when that data gets out? I don't know.

Charlie: — How the fuck do you not know? You just said it's possible.

Dylan: — But in order for any of this idea to occur. You will need a talented data extractor. Someone who can pull the data without error.

Lucy: — I know a guy... He just does that. But he does it on local data, he was part of the Slim Nets forensics... He could extract anything... Some said he could read the soul of the machine, performing an interrogation inside its circuits.

Charlie: — Where do we find him?

Lucy: — He's at Silverock.

Dylan: — Holy shit. What's a guy like that doing with these hardcore freaks?

Lucy: — He was from there. He was born and raised in Silverock before he joined the Slim Nets.

Charlie: — Let's go after him then.

Dylan: — There's one more thing.

Charlie: — What happened?

Dylan: — You know that friend of yours? Jeniffer? She's here with me...

Charlie: — Damn it Dylan. You came to tell me this only now?

Dylan: — I was hoping things would settle down with you

guys.

Charlie: — What the fuck... What the fuck.

Charlie snapped at Dylan holding the collar of his lab coat while Lucy held him: — Where is she? Where did you leave her man?

Lucy: — Calm down Charlie. Relax man. This way you won't achieve anything... Relax.

Dylan waited for Charlie to calm down... He got up, opened the door and said: — Come with me.

He led them into the other room of the apartment where she was lying with various devices on her body, it looked like she was hot-wiring her body. It was a mix between a car and a hospital room with gadgets to keep her breathing and dripping IVs.

Charlie approached where she was lying: — Jeniffer. What have these sick people done? They tore you apart.

Dylan: — I don't know how she managed to survive... I really don't.

There was a cloth on Jeniffer's ribs still in the wound between open, when Charlie got up to check Dylan spoke up: - Don't touch it there Charlie. I couldn't get a good fix on what she has in her system... That part was exposed.

Charlie lifted the cloth and saw that mechanical opening under the skin, you could still see inside, it wasn't the ribs, but an iron plate with a deep mark from a hole not penetrated in the steel... To the side that symbol of the number one with a square around... Charlie looking at that sighed of relief almost crying: —Jeniffer... You fucker. You didn't tell me you were using the Q1aY model... So you easily recognized that guy's model.

Lucy: — Model Q1aY?

Charlie: — It's an untraceable armor... A model of which she was very familiar.

Dylan: — Now I get it... But I still don't understand how she survived so many gunshots.

Charlie: — Her body must be totally armored with this stuff.

Dylan: — I found that near her, too.

Dylan withdrew the samurai sword from the corner of the room, the chrome gleaming in the light... Charlie took it and spoke sadly: — Mia's sword...

Dylan: — I just found the sword... And your friend.

Charlie tightened the scabbard of his sword: — Mia is gone... What the fuck... Those WeaponTech assholes are so fucked up on mine.

Lucy: — Charlie. We still have more things to do... Then we'll get them... Who controls them, we have to get them.

Charlie: — No. You don't understand. We're gonna get them all... Fuck WeaponTech, fuck Cybermind, and fuck them all... They're all fucked in mine. And whoever takes for them is gonna die too. It's fucking war now.

Lucy: — We have to be alive to catch these guys... That's why we have to go to Cybermind.

Charlie: — You're right... Now it's over... We're out of time.

Lucy: — Let's go then.

Charlie: — Come on. Dylan... Leave the sword near her... She knows what to do with it. I don't know anyone more skilled than her- Blowing up and cutting. That's what she does best.

Dylan: — Under my couch are some machine guns... You can take them. Arm yourselves heavily to go to those Silverock freaks.

Lucy: — Beauty. Leave it to us.

Charlie looked at Jeniffer: — Dylan. Do you take care of her? Take good care of her?

Dylan: — Don't worry. I'll stay here and take care of her. I'll do everything i can to keep her alive. And find a way to reverse this damage to you... But we need an extractor to link your data to Neurodatta.

Charlie: — Dylan. Thanks for rescuing us. Thanks for helping Jenifer. Without you we wouldn't be in this shit. But then again, we'd already be fucked.

Dylan: — I'm just trying to fix a mistake. I'm not gonna forgive myself for that... I'm looking at all this shit as redemption already.

Lucy: — We're going to need your help to get into Cybermind.

Dylan: — You can count on me... I'm with you... You can get my car; the key is on the table in front of the couch.

Then the three of them left the room, Dylan headed to the table to continue checking what could be done, while Charlie and Lucy grabbed the weapons from the couch. Each knew what they had to do... The way now was Silverock, to get to the Cybermind...

Nervousness was evident... The blood of fear made the steels cold... It was clear, to enter the most unpredictable place in Tech City only armed to the teeth... After all... It wasn't just any place... It was Silverock.

SILVEROCK

Shoot first ask questions later. That was the motto in Silverock, the cleanest place in Tech City. The white painted gates lived open in that neighborhood that looked more like a gated community. Only those who were from Silverock knew the law there... Only those who were welcome or already from there could get in. Everything was taken advantage of: every circuit, every wire, every blood, every component. The cleanest place in town, the biggest center of thieves in one place in the whereabouts of obscure and always unknown gangs, as if there was an underworld behind the underworld of crime.

They were pacts sealed in the shadows between people, so the gangs of anonymity were formed, no one knew to whom they belonged and with whom they were. All you could see for no reason was a car passing by and shooting some guys on the sidewalk during the Sunday barbecue. No one knew literally anything about Silverock's hidden crimes... It would be better to build a wall around it and let the animals kill each other.... That was a guy's idea once; the project came from a know-it-all alderman who wanted to call the shots, thinking he could call the shots just because he had a strong corporation on his back. He mysteriously died of poisoning inside his office with a note on his forehead that said. *"Don't mess with Silverock."* The crimes in that neighborhood were like that, full of mysteries, conspiracy theories and the most varied absurd speculations you could hear. Once it was confused on the radio, instead of being called the neighborhood of thieves. The journalist who was eager and crazy to win over someone's tragedy with destructive revelations, without wanting to reveal what no one had the courage to speak in public about what it was there, called it the neighborhood of professional killers... The end... Everybody already knew... It was a matter of time for him to die mysteriously.

Rifle aiming at the car where Charlie and Lucy were: — Are you aiming at them?

— Yes, I am.

— It won't kill. Shoot the tires, could be newbies around here.

— What's the matter? Did it soften?

Then the guy standing on top of the church took out his binoculars: — We're not on red alert... That must be Lucy. I'm not sure it's her. So don't hit anyone yet.

The car was coming calmly near the Silverock entrance when it was surprised by a shot in the tire, Lucy lost control of the car and had to brake near the gate by the right side of the sidewalk that connected the side of the gate: — What the fuck. Did you see that?

Charlie: — These guys are crazy. Coming in shooting like that... without knowing who it is... Now these shits will see.

By the time Charlie had pulled two pistols from his pants... Lucy touched his arm: — Wait a minute Charlie.

Then there came into Silverock that car with a family in it... Two kids in the back seat and a couple in the front... The man stopped the car: — Are you guys in need of a little help out there?

Lucy: — No. It's all right. It was just an accident.

— Imagine that. I insist.

Out came that neat man in the short-sleeved collared shirt and khaki pants... He had neat hair and a mustache, looking like he'd come from a TV commercial... He opened the trunk, got the car key and jack: — Do you have a spare tire?

Charlie: — Yes, I do...

Lucy kicked the tire while Charlie took the spare tire. Lucy greeted the woman in the driver's seat, who saw her turning back: — Children... Keep quiet.

Charlie: — I'll do it.

— No. Don't worry. I'll take care of it. I'll be glad to help you.

The man began by placing the jack and removing the wheel: — These things happen. Sometimes we hit some holes or they forget some component on the floor.

Charlie: — Yeah... These things happen.

Lucy: — Are you guys from around here?

The man then went about removing the wheel: — Oh yes. Yes, we are... Born and raised in Silverock.

Charlie: — Thank you so much for helping us change the tire... It's hard for a person these days to stop and help someone.

The man then took the spare tire and began to put it on: — Yes. Very difficult... This city needs more of this... More civility among citizens.

Lucy: — Rare things to have nowadays.

After changing the tire he kicked the tire a few times while removing the dirt from his hands with a cloth: — So. What are you guys doing here?

Lucy: — We came to find my friend.

— Do you have any friends around here?

Lucy: — We work together. I don't know if you know

him.

— This is a small neighborhood. Who is he? Maybe I know...

Lucy: — His name is Franklin.

— I think I know who it is.

The man turned and spoke to his wife: "Baby. Do you know any Franklin around here? That name is not unfamiliar to me.

She spoke loudly from the car: — Franklin? The boy from the five hundred and eleven? Kristen's son?

The man put the cloth in his pocket: — Ah yes... Franklin. Great kid.

Then he smiling ironically looked seriously into Lucy's eyes: — May I know what you want with him?

Lucy innocently spoke up: — It's private business.

Sensing in a subtle way Lucy's hostility, the man answered: — You are lucky. You received the first warning... Only one shot in the tire. Apparently they don't know where they are.

Charlie felt something different coming from the man's words, something was going to happen and he answered: — We are about to do a job. And we need his help with extraction... He is the best isn't he? He must be doing the data extraction jobs for you guys.

Looking at Charlie the man spoke up: — You know, you know about these things, don't you? These things of death...

Charlie: — So... Is he there?

The man looked into Charlie's eyes: — Yes... He's here.
Charlie: — Great.

— I'll take you there... Just wait a little while.

He put his finger to his ear and answered someone else on the other end of the line. *"It's okay... They're clean. You can put the rifle down... From now on leave it to me."*

Then he said to both of them: — You can come with me. It's all right. I will guide you to Franklin.

On the way to Franklin, Lucy spoke: — Strange. They always tell me it's an extremely violent neighborhood, that you should never come here alone. But look at these houses, all organized. It's like a little paradise in the middle of Tech City. Polite people, throwing water on the lawn, kids playing with their dogs in the yard, there's even an ice cream vendor around here. All very organized and clean... with top-quality implants all over their bodies... They're first line steel.

Charlie: — You don't know what they're about, do you? They're professional killers. They don't work for Tech City. Silverock is the place they just sleep. I've heard stories of some trouble around here... But they're just stories... They refuse to do business in Tech City. They don't work for anyone here... Only in other cities. A whole neighborhood of professional killers who do their work on the sly, surrounded by mystery everywhere. It's more sinister here than you can imagine. Everybody respects this place, nobody messes with them... And one story I heard, barroom stuff, is that they're forbidden to kill professionally in Tech City. It's a law around here. But not everybody complies, and I heard that if you don't comply with that rule they go after the guy, hunt the guy down in the depths of murder. No one here allows you to cross the line of the rules set among the assassins... Aren't you a first line hacker? Welcome to Silverock. The place of the first line assassins.

Lucy: — Franklin was born here I believe he came back because he trusts that this is the safest place in Tech City.

Charlie: — As far as I know you simply don't choose to live here. They're extremely territorial... Either you were born here, family thing. Or you're invited to live here.

That horn was heard in front of the five hundred in eleven. Lucy and Charlie saw some people from the neighborhood looking out the window... Franklin coming out of the house, greeting the man in the car... Lucy and Charlie got out of the car... Soon Franklin already spoke hugging Lucy: — Hello Lucy.

Lucy: — Hey Franklin... This is Charlie.

Charlie said hello: — What's up.

Franklin replied: — What's up.

Franklin was entering the house: — Come on... Come on in... You must be starving... I'll make something for you.

Charlie: — No need for me. Thanks.

Seeing Lucy dejected, Franklin soon spoke up: — What happened Lucy?

They sat on the couch in the living room and then she revealed everything to Franklin... The whole story, everything that happened... Until the moment came when he spoke: — I get it. So you need someone who can extract the information from inside you.

Charlie: — Exactly. We don't know if this is going to save us.

Franklin: — I think it might save... If it's just in the pulse system... It could break the binary accelerator, break the monochrome signal from the value recombination gate, changing the characteristics of the function classification, slowing down the information... That could be it.

Lucy: — How do you know that?

Franklin: — I know how to do recombination of numerical randomness, decomposing the post-binary structures of the cyberreck connected to the nervous system... Sometimes it happens that the information accelerates creating synaptic dysfunction, altering the chemical passages... It's in this middle of the road that the guys figured out how to make DeadReeper. The guys figured out how to connect the bits to the axons with electrodynamic impulse by defragmenting the nano capacitances of the central temporal leakage system.

Charlie: — So you're telling me you can help us? Fix this thing inside of us?

Franklin: — On the premise of this Dylan. It can be done... But for that to happen you have to be there.

Lucy: — That's the thing... We need someone to do the extraction. Dylan doesn't know about extraction. He knows about electro-informational systems and thermodynamic junction enhancements.

Franklin: — Got it. So you want me to go there.

Charlie: — We do.

Franklin: — You don't know Cybermind, do you? It's much more protected than WeaponTech.

Lucy: — As for the invasion. We now have two Slim Nets... We can break into the Cybermind.

Charlie: — Anything you say, I'll come out and shoot these motherfuckers.

Franklin: — The thing goes much further than that...

When you heard someone calling Lucy... Her biodisk calling... When she answered, she heard a female voice say: — Put it on the hologram there.

As they put it into the hologram... She, Charlie and Franklin saw Dylan's apartment, and him on his knees facing the camera, a few soldiers around... With Isabelle and Joshua, each with a pistol.

Isabelle: — I know you wouldn't come for someone who fucked you... That's why I'm doing you this favor.

That arm pointed the gun with such lightness that you could feel a synchronicity of death... She knew how to kill. That pressure of the pistol shot the fire at the tip, the flash that made the blood gush from Dylan's head. Flying short circuits from his head. Blood and components spilling onto the wall, that blue flash of the short circuit from his head already said it all... His soul was gone.

Joshua: — We can make a deal with you. We know that you are in the worst. We can save you. And in return we just want to know what's on your mind.

Isabelle: — Dylan told us all about it. We're curious how shit like that could end up in the heads of two fucked up assholes like you guys.

Joshua: — Your friend is with us... A fair exchange, don't you think?

Isabelle: — You know where to find us... When you're in the lobby... Sign in at the reception... It will be a friendly meeting.

Charlie: — Friendly... I know... Just like they did with Dylan.

Lucy: — How can we be sure you won't kill us?

Charlie: — How are we going to be sure they won't kill Jeniffer after we give them what they're after?

Joshua: — Come on. We're looking for what's inside you... That's all... What happened with dylan? It was internal. That's what a cheater deserves.

Isabelle: — Anything. Just think... Your friend is with us... If you want her back you'll have to come. There's no way.

Charlie: — We'll come over then... Just don't hurt her.

Joshua: — You have five days. If not I will assemble a new android with what's left of her body.

Isabelle: — We always need to assemble a robot to clean the floor... I think her parts will do the trick.

Charlie: — You sons of bitches... Don't touch her.

Joshua: — Then come to Cybermind... Don't make us wait... Five days... No more.

After the end of the call Charlie and Lucy were ready to invade the Cybermind, while Franklin analyzed everything coldly... A silence of anger and hatred reigned in the room, making the atmosphere tense until Franklin spoke: — Okay. Let me see what you have. - He stood up ready to help the two of them, his doubts had been solved in that moment when Dylan was killed. I want to take a look at you.

Leading them towards an all-white corridor with white LEDs underneath the corridor and up on the ceiling ridges... Reaching a blue light on the wall he typed in a code and they walked down the stairs to his monitoring base... Containing several camera screens all around Silverock with the standard chair to do body system analysis. A dark room filled with red led's around the bench with apparatus, around the chair, ceiling and some spots lit up, that red lights went up the corners of the stair steps. Until he spoke: — Lucy. Sit there... Let's see what's in there.

Sticking the plug in the back of Lucy's head he didn't know what was waiting on the screen; he pulled a transparent screen to him with red lights on the letters... He touched some points in the screen and then he pulled another support with the keyboards... He typed and analyzed, Charlie looking at that pile of codes being swept out of Lucy's head.... They were lighting up Franklin's face in the darkness of what was left of the room... So, he relaxed, lowered his head and listened to Franklin: — Hey. How did you guys do that?

Lucy in the chair frightened in the chair spoke: — What is it?

Franklin continued typing in disbelief: — I thought the parade had been simpler. I didn't think it was of such complexity.

Charlie continued looking at Franklin, noticing his startled countenance, he continued typing and said: — It has an informational pulse merged with the source of the biodirectional conductor, with each pulse it weakens the implantative immune system, it is a safety system designed pro body not to reject the bioelectric implants in the nervous system. You will feel an organic pain with the steel tearing your skin, but the body will fight pain, so you will feel strong headaches and vertigo from image duplication. I think it can be reversed, but I'll need a higher precision charge to acquire massive processing power, if the process is slow, you'll die... To mess with this I need the Suggestionizer that replaces the artificial work of the processors, and with it I can make a dichotomous link between the root of the electrobiomechanical force with the acceleration of the binding of the bits of the neuroconnections. But I need to be there to interconnect with their information and use what they have inside the data cracks to be able to reverse the informational pulse process... But...

Noticing the change in Franklin's expression, Charlie gives an automatic response: — What happened?

Franklin: — My Suggestioner was stolen when they broke into our Slim Nets headquarters.

Lucy: — I don't believe it... You're telling me that to get the Suggestionizer. Maker we'll need to break into the Foxyes' headquarters.

Charlie was scared shitless when he heard that name, to mess with those faggots was something that could not be turned back: — Were you guys mad at the Foxyes?

Franklin: — Not only them... Several gangs got together to get us... But they were the guys who cleaned up our headquarters

Charlie: — Fuck... These sickos will trade anything... Mechanical remains of people, electrical components, stolen prostheses, I learned that they even have fresh bodies to remove the implants with one hundred percent of utilization. If you pass out on the street and they are around, you can kiss your legs and arms goodbye; that's if they don't take your head too to take advantage of the improvements to your eyes and ears. I don't know if your stuff will be with them. More than sure that what you had is already in the hands of others.

Lucy speaking as she lay back in the chair with a plug in the back of her head: — I'm not sure Charlie... Anyone who had what we had would have a lot of advantages in a lot of things. The stuff we had, they wouldn't want to sell.

Thoughtfully looking serious as he pulled the plug out of the back of Lucy's head, Franklin spoke up: — We're going to have to go over there.

Lucy: — What the fuck... It's still too early...

Franklin: — Were you planning on it too?

Lucy: — I was... I was planning to get all of them... Everyone who participated in that massacre... But something like that takes time. If we attack them now, the others might change their headquarters or leave town. I'm not sure they'll do that. They may be overconfident and think we can't handle it.

Franklin: — I've been talking to some hackers who were working with us; there were some rumors on the net that anarchy was planned... Everyone who got in trouble that day started making the same plans we did.

Lucy: — I wonder if we can get help from them.

Franklin: — You know there's no way. Everyone there worked as a tribe, all of ours were wiped out... The guys that are left from the Slim Nets are working alone or in groups of the ones that are left, all under the covers to not be discovered, it's very difficult to communicate... I can't find anyone. It's just rumors in codes that are impossible to be traced, left in the hatchets of the networks, a kind of secret code behind the tracks... But from the looks of it... If we attack, they might attack other places in the next few days, I don't know, they were just rumors of codes in the middle of digital shadows... A way we found to leave coding symbols, between lies and truths, a kind of conspiracy illusion impossible to believe... But sometimes we get something good to know, and everyone's afraid to see themselves... And be just another trap victim.

Lucy: — You don't know how relieved I am to hear that Franklin.

Franklin: — I had hopes too.

Lucy sitting up in her chair looked into Franklin's eyes with a short half sad, half hopeful smile: — We can try.

Franklin: — We can.

Charlie got up and the three of them stood facing each other amidst those red LED lights on the floor and ceiling of the dark room... It was the semblance, the silhouette of the three looking at each other and finding a final solution followed by hope to solve the problem of all at the same time... Soon Charlie spoke: - Let's go for it... Let's get the Foxyes, get the Suggestionizer, and recover from the damage the Cybermind did to us.

FOXYES

It was night, it was raining, neither hard nor soft; was the water so shallow that it looked like fire drops passing through the city's leds like comets falling from the sky. But not all the water in the world could clean up the dirt in Tech City. That filth coming from the extremities of power, a sewer of pure violence and corruption, gangs seeking an illusory respect and corporations knowing how to take advantage of this violence... It was profitable to sell to all sides, no matter which it was, the business was to have loyal customers ready to make up.

The Foxyes gang had their operational HQ in a concrete shed with old factory checkered windows, commercial sliding garage gate at the entrance next to the open yellow container, graffitied walls on both sides with several cameras around the place. Some metal boxes, some sealed chemical tanks in the yard. And a blue-green Speedvypper car, lowered with a pointy beak, big wheels, with the rear covered with orange red LEDs continuous horizontal from one end to the other, inside the car glowing green by the LEDs that made luminous highlights on the dark windows. Only four guys could be seen in front of the Foxyes headquarters with machine guns.

They had cybernetic prosthetics implanted in their arms and two of them had metallic eyes coupled with orange LEDs. You could see the chrome steels on the arms of the guys dressed in leather hooded sweatshirts... The gang's audacity was so big that they even had a logo on top of the gate, a kind of orange led facade of a fox with one paw up analyzing, its paws not only had the leds design, but also chrome steel with red horizontal faded traces of car rear brake light plastic.

Sneaking up through the wall and right on top of Charlie's container with his silenced pistol, he could feel the sound of water on the tin near him and further on the water hitting the leather of his sweatshirts. While having that mixture of sounds of water hitting the tiles and floor, causing a steam to rise from the asphalt, he heard Franklin's voice on the radio "*It's okay. I was able to turn the cameras off,*

Charlie paused to listen to Lucy: — Do they have this parade around here?

Franklin: — Are you thinking what I'm thinking?

Lucy: — It has to be him... Only he knows about these things.

Charlie on the wire not understanding: — Who are you talking about?

Franklin: — Bitwolf.

Lucy: — A Slim Net of our own... Don't you remember what I told you Charlie? It's more dangerous with the first line hackers out there.

Franklin: — Tell me about it... I wonder if he's here.

Lucy: — I don't think so... He's the kind of guy who puts it together and shaves it off.

Lucy behind the wall with a rifle with silencer and bendable barrel, dripping from the tip of the rifle, a different system, able to see the other side of the wall and be able to shoot through the wet camera of the rain: — Okay... I've got the left one in my sights.

Charlie moved closer so he could hack the second guy's mind from right to left... His eyes shone to the sparkling blue: — I'm coming in... Hold there.

He on top of the container with those eyes gleaming blue, crouching and holding the pistol with silencer in the dark of night while the water was falling.... They were hunter's eyes chasing their prey watching from up there from the back as the three of them talked without caring what was going on.

As he invaded his mind... Lucy's eyes turned flickering pink invading the other guy's mind, if she could see her little in that dark through the far city lights, her eyes stood out, propped on the pinched cement wall, watching the bluish screen of the rifle making a flash her face, the bent barrel with one arm bent on top of the wall amidst the darkness of that rain... The three were getting ready to attack while listening the guys' conversations through the Dinamo-Stereo system that amplified directly the sound to a point.

The guy on the left: — So what did you say?

Second from left to right: — I told you the truth. You want your arm back? You have until tomorrow to put the Neurocoin in the account, or else you'll be scrap metal.

Guy from the right: — He fell for that?

— Guys always fall for it. They think they're getting something fancy, something first class, but it's just the same shit used from the corpses we fry.

The guy on the left: — That's the law. Late payment, you lose your arm.

Second from right to left: — Did he pay you?

Second from left to right: — No way. He gave me a few bucks saying that was all he had and he would pay the rest next week.

The guy on the right: — What's up? What's up?

— I stole his other arm and sold them both for half price to another crazy... That's what happens when you want to buy cold shit without a gun... The chance of getting fucked up is always high.

The guy on the left: — Do not get involved with this shit man... These outside with farm parts only gives problems.

— Now it's just supplying the third party guys... You cannot pass the crap on staff.

The guy on the left: — Remember Teddy? He went to sell Hotchips to the sluts in the Pussypink gang... Those chips that make the pussy hot and they make the guy come faster, increasing the production of fuck in the day...

The guy on the right: — I got it.

The guy on the left: — The shit was farm... Shit happened, the mines started electrocuting the guys dicks. The whole fucking thing went to space. They got fucked up pretty good... They lost some heavy clients...

Second from left to right: — And what happened?

The guy on the left: — They beat him to death in an alley... He was punched and kicked until the circuits shorted out.

— What a crazy guy. He went and messed with Pussypink right away.

Guy on the left: - I think I could roll... With a kamikaze gang like theirs you cannot play and sell junk farm... We have to get the first class stuff, like we do for third parties and get some credibility credits for the next sale.

The guy from right to left: — When the shit is hot, they always come back.

Charlie on the radio: — I broke his cryptodisk... I'm in.

Lucy: — I also entered... Just give the signal.

Charlie: — Now.

Everything was synchronized at the same time. The two hacked guys shorted out quickly, internally bursting their minds, blood coming out, sparks coming out of their eyes and ears... Blood in their mouths when they opened from momentary pain... It was too fast, it only gave them time to put their hands on their heads from the extreme pain and black out right there.... At the same time they stormed in, Charlie fired with the silencer pistol at the back of the second guy's head from left to right, sparks, components and blood came out of his forehead. Charlie spoke *"Good night"*.

The guy on the left felt the pressure of the bullet penetrating his temple, there was no time for anything, the body fell hard to the side, it was a quick and accurate shot, opening a hole on both sides of his head followed by sparks - Lucy then added *"Time for a nap"*. There were four of them lying crooked on the floor bathed in a pool of blood in front of the Foxyes headquarters.

Lucy jumped the wall and invaded through the corner and Charlie through the other side... Inside it was a mixture of orange LEDs from the equipment boxes, dim light bulbs on the ceiling making the atmosphere almost dark and screens passing data in light blue continuously... Some things were loose around the shed; it seemed empty and nobody in sight. They got closer to the middle and heard some very loud stepping noises coming from the bottom up, they were hidden behind the crates, and behind a crate there was a secret staircase where two guys climbed.

Charlie on the other side of the shed said on the radio: — What do you have there?

Lucy: — I have nothing... Discharged.

Charlie: — I still have one more... It's the blackout. I'm gonna have to use it. Did you see the size of this nutcase? He's got some fucking armor on his head. Did you call?

Lucy: — Use that... Let's see what it is.

One of them walked with a rifle and the other was two meters tall, a wall of technoprotein-enhanced muscles, a giant who spoke in a thick voice: -Did you get the signal? We lost contact with the guys.

— We're on alert, everybody's on.

Lucy on the radio: — What the fuck...

Franklin on the radio: — Bitwolf you sick bastard. What have you done? Implanted the shared Lookoff in the guys.

Lucy on the radio: — Now they know about us.

Charlie on the radio: — There's no way to wait for them to pass... They'll catch us on the way back.

Charlie started hacking, his eyes shone and at this moment the big guy took the pistol and pointed to the partner next door who spoke: — What the fuck is this guy? What the fuck are you doing?

— *I can't... Ah! Fuck!*

The shot was heard in the guy's head and he fell on the ground with a hole in his head, eyes turned upwards... The big guy took the pistol and aimed at his own head, kind of lowering his head... Coupling the barrel in a vulnerable and sensitive part of his head... A place that only he knew... He yelled a few more times, "*Ahh! What the fuck? Holy shit! AAhh!!!*. And pulled the trigger leaving a lot of blood and sparks from his head to the point of spurting in the air. Falling all crooked on the ground while you could see the footprints on the side passing through his body.... It was Charlie and Lucy going to the stairs... Full of orange lights on the steps that went down to a dark place....

Descending with caution and saw something never seen before... There were several people... Men, women and children submerged in various green water glasses on both sides of the hallway to the room at the back. The lights on top of the containers showed that they were being preserved to have their pieces used. Some moved as if they were dreaming, they were eternal sleeps in a parallel reality, wires attached to the back of their heads while their bodies floated upright in the water.

They had two screens, one facing the other in the central part passing data in light blue... Sometimes a red central line would pass, as they quickly showed the dreams being modified.

Lucy looked terrified: — What is it?

Charlie watching: — What a bunch of sick fucks. Look at that thing under each glass... Fucking What the fuck is this shit here? This shit right here?

At this moment he crouched down and ran his hand over the embossed writing on a plastic glued below the woman's feet. And it was written *"Summer Harvest"*: - Bunch of sons of bitches. They're making people into crops.

Lucy: — I'm going to see what they have in those machines... Those computers must be connected to their stain bank... If they used the Suggestionizer I'll be able to find it around here... It's a shadow of their internal cloud that records all the usage logs of the devices You can hack into it.

Charlie: — Where are all these people connected?

Lucy at the computer complemented Charlie's speech — You won't believe it Charlie... The thing is much worse than we are seeing ... They are all in a dualistic reality within the Texture, connected together with the Textures of the people of the city... A copy of our reality in a world in pre-cybernetic civilization, a lot of people are addicted to this, have a whole life in this shit, and barely know they share intimacies with people who are already physically dead, kept by the brain inside canned water, just the body waiting to be used in a cybernetic implant. It's a world just like real life, but out here they're zombies wandering around after easy scams, just to keep the addiction in there. And there are people who earn a lot of Neurocoin inside this metareality, while they bathe in the money, others deposit the only time they have, the last breath of life of their realities to maintain the constancy of utopian perfection built in their own idealistic world...

Lucy as she typed continued: — These Texture addicts no longer care about reality, for it is cruel.... More cruel than ever, all unreality transformed into a violent and chaotic reality. No one could take it, Texture turned out to be the new cocaine. Smelling unreality to keep the heart beating in the little time left in this world... They are not lost and neither lost, only won, nobody wants to lose, only to win, this is the payment in who lives of unreality, the base of his addiction, the nectar of the opium... To win... And they leave there wanting that here it is equal, they hurry, they act hasty, finally they transform it here into something much worse than it already is... The utopia of unreality has transformed reality into a field of elysiums covered with hypocritical flowers stained by the blood of the chains of violence. Multitasking performance is a sand-covered nothingness about to crumble on top of our heads.... It is what we are. An accelerated life, dead in illusory time.

Charlie looking at the bodies in the water: — We are just in the rest of our civilization...

Lucy: — This unreal dream of Texture is a pre-cybernetic life... It's about that time... That's when the digital age began to emerge Poor things; they barely knew what they were waiting for. That big war that fucked everything up and they had to speed up the whole process and go full digital for good.

Charlie: — I remember well, they thought they were too evolved to understand the flow of data, not understanding that this flow would turn against them when artificial intelligences started cross-referencing faulty data... penetrating all military structures... They could have reversed that politicized dissonance shit that was fucking with people's heads. Penetrated into delusional idealism, believing in an ideal and barely connecting that they were all being monitored by themselves.

Lucy: — Until there was the nuclear bomb of information. Nobody knows where it started from, who did it...

Charlie: — Don't you remember Lucy the stories they always tell? It was the faulty data breaches of the artificial intelligences... They started building fake duplicates and the security ones attacking themselves.... There was the biggest shit nobody could have imagined... The biggest widespread data leak in the world. All the data in the world was leaked. Private conversations, groups, accesses and all the sensitive information of the intelligence agencies... Exabytes of servers with headphone and camera recordings spied on twenty four hours a day... Everything for everyone to see... Every eye saw... It was a general civil war. The first anarchist manifesto through exposed data... No one wanted to accept that other people were talking nonsense about them in private conversations on smartphones.

Lucy: — They were very innocent... They believed in a centralized cybernetics.

Charlie then stood up and lit a cigarette: — We are nothing more and nothing less than the reflection of our innocence.

Lucy: — Innocence lived in irreversible times.

Charlie took a puff of smoke from the canned body in front of him: — Welcome to our age... The age of dreams... The cybernetic age.

Lucy: — I got it... The device is still here. It was used yesterday in an organ exchange to keep the bioelectric system active in the body. I found where it is. They didn't take it off their computer.

Charlie: — Let's go over there then...

Lucy: — On the second staircase...

Charlie: — Go lower?

Lucy: — Come on.

Charlie and Lucy went to the end of the corridor and bending to the left they saw other open rooms with cameras pointed to some bodies missing parts, people in bathtubs, piles of electronic components, parts on the floor... Tool cabinets... And some rooms had cut plastics with heads, legs and arms cybernetic in garbage cans... Cybernetically torn open bodies in dental chairs... Some bodies with wires integrated from the ceiling.... The rooms were dimly lit with several thick wires in the ceiling.

Charlie: — Holy shit... The guys have done a tremendous amount of carnage here.

Lucy: — This is almost cybernetic cannibalism... I can't believe they take leftovers from people like that. Like that without caring about anything.

Charlie: — I don't know how you got mixed up with these people... These guys are sick. Did you see that shit over there? That camera? Someone should buy some footage of people being disassembled, watch a little death by implant removal.

Lucy: — The sicker ones still increase with audience the sickness of the guys.

Charlie: — They must enjoy choking themselves watching

these death movies.

Lucy: — Yeah... These guys are not messing around.

Going down the stairs they came across a large open room of constructions to do, wood, lamps and some boxes with components thrown... Several construction woods to assemble and divide rooms, another ladder beside to go down another floor... And in the background some lights... As they were getting closer that light was getting stronger, the two of them with their guns pointed getting closer, seeing a room on the right with several appliances on the floor with wires on the ceiling, followed by computers having numbers passing quickly on the screens. She pointed to the room and spoke: - It's here.

On the left side a room with cement some cameras and lights pointed to a mattress on the floor, it seemed to be a person lying down, sleeping with his hands tied and chain in the left leg attached to the floor. When they got closer they realized that it was a woman sleeping, her long beige dress was out of place among the lights near the cameras... Noticing a certain approach she woke up, looked at them speaking between tears and blurred makeup: "Please. Help me. They put me here.

Lucy: — Calm down. We're going to get you out of there.

Charlie: — Fuck. What would these crazy people do?

The woman replied: — They said they were going to film me dying and that this would give them good money... Then they hit me and I fainted.

Lucy cut the metal clamps that held the woman's hands while Charlie tried to see a way to get those chains off her leg, soon he spoke: — It's going to be okay.

At that moment they hadn't realized that the lights on the mattress indicated only one thing... Easy prey to fall into the trap. Noises were heard coming from the slack ceiling, falling several women and heavily armed men, reaching over every corner of that floor... Noises of machine guns, rifles and pistols triggering, ready to burn and finish with the two... They heard those voices.

— It's party time.

— Uh-oh! Two more for the fridge.

— There. I'll take those snazzy eyes of hers, huh?

— Fuck Asshole I was going to ask for the eyes of mine... So okay, I'll take the guy's arms.

— Let's make some good money... Prepare the tools.

Charlie and Lucy turned around aiming to defend the woman, pointing the gun at everyone there And the woman standing on their backs stood up with her eyes flashing red and two spears sticking out of the side of her arms, the chrome steel glinting in the darkness of the blades made them look back to the point where Charlie pointed the pistol to her while Lucy pointed the rifle to the rest of the guys. Then they heard the woman's voice: "Do you think it's all right to come and fuck with us? We smelled cold from far away.

The voice of someone from that crowd: — Amateurs.

Another voice: — Hey, boss. Let's fry their steel A little fun for today, then we'll sell the rest that's left.

The woman with red eyes and spears exposed from the sides of her arms spoke: — No, no. They are being sought by a group of people there. I've already contacted my contact to come get them... It's gonna be big money.

Charlie then spoke: — You fucking bitch... You set this whole thing up, didn't you?

Lucy: — She put six guys as bait... What do you think they are to her? Just bait, she'll use you guys too.

They heard a woman's voice in the middle of the armed crowd: — They were six assholes, they deserved to die... If they were smarter they would have caught you.

Charlie began to get dizzy... Feeling a strong headache, there was a heat rising tearing through his flesh, heating the steel in his body. Seeing things half double, a little blue and red at the same time, he dropped the pistol and put his hands on his head saying: — Fuck. What the fuck kind of pain is that?

Lucy pointing her rifle looked back asking: — What?   Charlie: — What the fuck... What a pain.

Lucy: — Calm down...

At that very moment Lucy also felt a strong headache, seeing the same things as Charlie.

She dropped the rifle crouching down and feeling a strong headache: — Holy shit. What's this? What the fuck is happening to us?

The woman, head of the Foxyes has spoken: — Do not interfere... Let them feel the pain.

Laughter was heard and some people cheered, some of them with rifles propped on their shoulders. Enjoying that pain of the two of them. And they both started to feel more pain, getting on their knees and almost screaming in pain. *"AHH!!!"* *"WHAT THE FUCK!!!"*

Some began to approach and kick the two, were kicks in the stomach, face and legs... And more and more they felt pain, almost did not feel the kicks of such a headache that palpitated their circuits. Until in a sudden moment there was an electromagnetic explosion reverberating in all corners that dispersed all around. At this, everyone around the two of them had shorted out their systems. They were blood with sparks coming out of their eyes, small explosive shorts on their chests, some legs fell short, others lost their arms and the woman who was behind them all shattered in several parts as if she was imploding and exploded from inside her body, making her blades attached to her arms jump hitting the walls. The weapons crashed... It was heard some breaking glasses of the corridor where they were the people being conserved under water in the glasses... A music was strongly heard in synchrony of the continuous noises, a strong sound in straight line with the mixture of several sounds in straight line, they were the sounds of the lack of heartbeat indicating the death of several of these people that were being kept.

After that pain they both passed out...

***

When they woke up, they had a different feeling... A sense of relief, a weight off their heads. As they got up they saw all the gang members dead and in pieces... There were arms on top of feet, legs on top of trunks, weapons bent, weapons dismantled, flesh mixed with electronics and steel. A pool of blood all around with eyes turned to every corner, silence, the sound of death hovering in an absolute continuity of lifelessness in all its electrifying essence.

Blood dripping from the ceiling with drips falling on the face of the corpse, electrocuted arms moving with short circuits, some bodies without faces, some without heads, and some Foxyes with exposed flesh, and underneath all that torso exposure you could see the crumpled metal, looking like ripping grooves. The pressure was so strong that the bodies couldn't take it to the point of imploding.

Charlie scared and at the same time relieved. He took a cigarette and lit it with the lighter; you could hear the sound of fire burning the paper in nicotine and then the sound of metal of the lighter closing. He took a drag and spoke as the smoke was rising: — Manufacturing defect.

Lucy: — We almost got away.

Charlie: — I don't know about you. But I thought I was going to die.

Lucy: — We had no way out... This shit that is killing us saved us.

Charlie: — It's... The curse that makes the witch a hero for saving the lost rabbit in the enchanted land.

Charlie and Lucy went to the tables where the devices were. The strangest thing was that only the people and gun lacerated, the equipment remained intact as if it was possible to have a pulse directed at targets.

Charlie: — Don't you find it strange that only the guys died and the guns destroyed but the rest of that room was left intact?

Lucy: — I found the whole fucking thing too weird man.

The two of them heard some broken voices, it was him trying to communicate, squeaks that slowly returned to normal sound. Franklin reestablishing the lost signal after the pulse: — What happened there? I lost the signal with you guys.

Charlie: — It fucked up. But we managed to solve it.

Lucy: — I got it here; I was able to get the Suggestionizer plug out of their system.

Charlie: — Go.

Franklin: — No. You don't understand.

The squeaking noise became even louder... It was hard to hear Franklin, only remnants of his voice could be heard. In this period the two went up the stairs unarmed, passing through the rooms, not finding any weapons along the way. Until they reached the floor above after the two stairs... As they went up the squeak of Franklin's voice faded, in this period the two saw the weapons of the dead men on the first floor, the guys Charlie hacked to shoot himself. She with a rifle and he with a pistol, in this period the sound returned to normal with Franklin's desperate speech: — *Get the fuck out of there now! The rest of the gang is coming!*

They moved those lights closer to the cars in the driveway, one of the cars even came to blow up the lights passing over the dead bodies of the four guys in front. They came to burn the intruders mercilessly. As they hit those hard brakes, you could hear the noise of doors slamming and guns rattling... There were a total of five cars full of guys armed to the teeth. One of them with chrome arms, machine gun pointed up with his right hand, brown leather pants and green tank top entering the shed: — The signal interrupted down there... It's time to kick some ass.

— Who had the audacity to kill the boss?

— A lot of audacity... That son of a bitch will pay dearly for it.

Charlie and Lucy propped up behind the crate near the stairs, scared to see that many people ready to hunt them down. That was a moment of certainty, where the death beat with more force the cold steel of dread. There was nowhere to run... Walking down only indicated a delay in the inevitable... At this exact moment when the gang was entering the shed, saw lights from the sky, a car in the skies to the air turbine with someone's voice in the speakers: — Put your guns down or we'll have to shoot.

The gang turned ready to fire, other guys leaned on the walls ready for the clash until loud noises of large caliber machine guns were heard shooting at the gang guys. The bullets were piercing through the guys, gushing blood on the blunts of their bodies, the propped up guys didn't stand a chance, the bullets went through the walls, they were tracer bursts piercing everything in front of them. The gang couldn't even fight back, everyone was shot without forgiveness, the deal was to finish the job right there, without witnesses.

Until the shots ceased and only the sound of the cylindrical iron of the bearings of the revolving machine guns was heard, the sound of the ropes being raised and lowered. Arriving the guards covered, reinforced vests and helmets with machine guns entering with everything, positioned strategically, each one watching from a different side. Lucy seeing all that asked: — What the fuck is going on?

Charlie: — Archive burning... They were just waiting for the guys to arrive to finish off the Foxyes once and for all.

Lucy: — Could it have something to do with the contact their leader talked about?

Charlie: — Could be.

It could be seen in total evidence that the place was dominated, several guards, each one in its strategic shooting point while that guy approached, his silhouette was mysterious passing through the lights of the cars. It was him... Joshua with shimmering red colored eyes, lab coat and a pistol in his hand. He arrived shooting the head of the guy in the green regatta who was crawling, a loud bang in the shed and blood from the head splattering on the floor: — The pulse signal came from here... They must be close by.

IT'S NOW

A while passed and nothing... Just soldiers lost between the doubt and the wound of unplanned self-confidence during the endless search, some wanted to feel the sadistic adventure of death in the normal rhythm of the city while others couldn't stand the massive tramp and the business was to stay in the good. The bodies were still there lying on the ground like meaningless junk trash about to be recycled, one guy walked up the third staircase and spoke loudly: — Nothing here.

Meanwhile two soldiers were talking as they walked down the corridor where the bodies were being preserved in glass. A man and a woman with machine guns and dressed in Cybermind uniform and helmet. Soon he spoke: — Where are those fucking crazies?

She replied: — They evaporated on that fucking wrist.

— Did you see the bodies down there?

— I wanted to be here to see the shit blow up.

— You hear what they're saying?

— I've heard some pretty lame shit from those two.

— What? How far do you know?

—A bitch that moves like a bullet, able to enter the body of the guys. And a terrorist who evaporated in the information and lives like a ghost walking through walls... Just like the guy in Cybermind.

In a voice of debauchery he asked: — Do you believe in ghosts?

She replied in a convinced voice: — I believe in murderers.

— I don't really know... Maybe... Look what's going on at Cybermind... He's even got a signature on the bodies. Man... I think it might be a ghost thing...

— All right. A ghost would do that to those guys.

During their walk the pair began to slow their steps as they talked. With that, he spoke: — That Foxyes gang are sick.

Soon she answered: — They pay very well for a body in great condition... And even more in conserved enhancements.

— What don't you do to stay alive in this shitty town?

— That's not all their income is... They had a brilliant idea.

He then looked half crossed as he listened: — Is it?

— Don't you see the plugs on their necks? What do you think they are? They're live bots in Texture.

He: — Pure shit. Live bots? I've heard about it. But I thought it was just rumor, or something in my head that I thought was insane and didn't believe.

— They are living, organic bots in the cyberspace of metareality, augmenting the territoriality of place with locals and audience legitimately built by Texture artificial intelligence system. It recognizes the difference between living and artificial organism, but does not recognize a harvest.

He: — Harvest?

She: — Have you never heard of it? People kidnapped to keep a double crop... One to be torn apart and one for cyberspace... You can have one inside your house if you want.

He: — I didn't know that.

She: — So they gain an audience, control some actions of these live bots and increase their content productivity. Making a hefty profit.

He: — And nobody wakes up?

She: — There's no way... They only wake up when they go under the knife.

Him: — The sweet old reality.

She: — Reality is illusion with pain   For those who pay for the sins of being living in it. As for unreality? She is sweet in a world disintegrated by space that lets life pass by   A desert with no taste, no smell and no color... About to lose its sand to the wind of time. Who likes reality? Did you see those bodies down there? Who wants to be there?

— I think I got it. That's why there's no way they can get out of Texture. They spend their whole lives in it.

— You know... I envy them. At least they make decisions for themselves. Bodies programmed to live inside an unreality built to grind their minds.

— I still think they're poor bastards who didn't ask to be where they are.

— None of us did.

At this moment of discussion he ran his hand over the dusty glass looking in and seeing that body in a deep trance of unreality. The green of the lights above with the reflection of the green of the waters highlighting his face being seen from inside the glass... At this, something approached the glass, slowly went up quietly inside the water, until leaning the gun barrel on his forehead through the glass... Then a flash of fire rolled in that caused the glass to shatter, blowing the guy's mind. The body fell by the curiosity, bullet preserved, blood that splashed on his partner's helmet and gushed on the front glass... Soon, the glass began to fall forward while the naked guy inside twisted to get out with his feet from the top... During his fall a guard at the beginning of the corridor started to shoot the glass... Green water was coming out of the shots between the holes and pieces of glass.

The guard, the guy's partner, started shooting the glass... But the guy inside it had already come out the other side. When the glass fell on the corpse, out came that man rolling, crouching and shooting the pistol hitting a bullet on her neck, stretched the arm pro other side and shot hitting the guy's neck at the beginning of the corridor... It was him Charlie.

From the place that had the piles of bodies was heard a cry *"Fuck! He's around here!* ". A guy was running towards the corridor, when in his back, inside the pile of bodies, arms, heads and legs. Appeared the barrel of that rifle bathed in blood that was rising along with her, Lucy. Firing on the guy's back. The body flew forward with everything, sound of plastic breaking; it was the helmet crashing into the pillar with the force of the body.

Naked Charlie started shooting and walking down the hallway that had the cybernetic leftover junk. One guy leaned on the wall and spoke: — Fuck. They're using Gmirror... That's why we can't identify them.

When he got up to shoot he got shot in the head, so did another guy who went up the ladder and got shot in the neck, coming down the ladder near the squad that was suffering rifle shots from Lucy. It was bullets coming from above and below.... It was not a gunfight, but a meat grinder. Massacre was set in the end of hope for those who imagined living another day in Tech City.... Faces up with suffering and pain of the bullets penetrated the bodies, screams of lost soldiers, blood splattering up, short circuits in the frantic mixture between blood and electronics. That face on the ground with half the helmet no longer existed; a part was ripped off in the purest brutality.... Charlie shot from up there while Lucy shot from down there, a new fashion, the art of the time, a stair made of bodies, bodies that piled up and down. Caught off guard and massacred at the right moment.

From up there the soldiers with their guns pointed at the stairs could hear only the soldiers' gunshots and shouts. *"He's here!"*. And sounds of machine gun fire. *"Cover me!"*. *"Go! Go, go, go! Go!"*. Rifle shots, a pause. And then two pistol shots, machine gun short, missed shots. *"Fuck! He fell!"*. *"Fuck you, motherfuckers!"* *"Is that what you want? You want my soul?"* Machine gun fire louder and louder. A rifle shot. *"Ah Sons of bitches... My leg!!! Ahhh."**"Hold on man... Hold on!"*. Sound of groaning pain as bursts of machine gun fire alternated in followed by responses from the pistol and rifle. *"I don't think so. He's gone!"*. *"Over here! Over here!"*. Machine gun sounds... You could see flashes of light down the stairs and the noise increased. That's when they heard that scream *"Don't fucking shoot! It's us! We're coming up!"*. Scary rifle shots with the bang on the wall in front of the stairs. A soldier left throwing himself with the other on the side. After they made it up the stairs, the guy carried his partner who was limping in pain.

Both were holding machine guns in one hand, one soldier was carrying the other with a limp; both had their helmets covered in blood... Then the guy who was carrying said: — They're coming...

At this point in the conversation the two were quickly passing the rest of the six soldiers who were getting ready, some standing and others on their knees, all with machine guns pointed.... The injured guy propped himself up next to Joshua and his private security guard approached speaking: — What's up... How are you?

The soldier who was putting the other sitting on the floor said: — It's fucked up, man.

— Let me see that wound there.

At this moment a noise began to be heard on the stairs... Something rising slowly... When they saw it was a guy dragging himself, stretching his arm and raising his head giving his last breaths. It was when the security guard pulled up one leg of his pants asking: — What's up... How are you? A lot of pain?

At this moment he couldn't see any gunshots. The guy sat down and pulled his pistol from his holster, saying in a feminine voice: — Not as much pain as you're going to feel.

The pistol shot out from under his chin, blood pouring out over his head... The brains coming out, splattering upwards. With that pistol bang, the others looked back, not understanding the situation. The guy who carried shot hitting the back of the head of the guy in front who fell instantly, the blood gushed on the helmet of the soldier in front who was standing... Who was hit in the back of the knees, then as he fell on the top of his head. The soldier who turned around took a shot in the face to the point of dismantling the front of his helmet. The others on the other side took shots in the chest and face, falling like dominoes.... And so they went down one by one It was echoes of trapping that were being made in the soldiers' last hope of getting out of there alive. At this moment Joshua a little far away started to run, and the person who was sitting down aimed right and hit a shot behind the leg and grazed. Making Joshua fall and at the same time he fell, he turned around pointing his gun, the standing soldier shot his pistol, making it loose from his hands.

Joshua lay frightened seeing those two who walked towards him removing their helmets... It was them Charlie and Lucy... With blood stains on their faces looking at Joshua through the lights of the shed... Approaching him and pistol- whipping him in the forehead, putting him to sleep.

A NEW REALITY

Joshua's eyes were still cloudy, being placed and tied with steel wires on his arms facing backwards. Soon he received a slap from Charlie: — Wake up.

Lucy: — Slap him some more... We need him awake to get the data.

On the radio Lucy talking to Franklin. *"Are you in my biodisk?"*. *"I'm in, just plug it in."*

Lucy then takes the plug wire from her wrist, from the top of her closed hand and spoke to Franklin. *"Plugged in."* Franklin replied. *"Okay. I'm going in."*

Charlie to Joshua: — Did you think it was just like that? Just come here and get us?

Joshua: — It was only a matter of time before the pulse appeared in the system and found you.

Charlie: — Yeah, but you're the ones who took it up the ass.

Joshua: — Your time is coming. It's coming for all of us... You are only prolonging the inevitable.

Charlie then lit a cigarette turning sideways looking at nothing and spoke: — It doesn't matter who goes from this to better, at some point we are all going to die... What matters is that others die before us.

Joshua: — That's the spirit of Tech City. The dream only ends in the one who knows death.

Charlie: — You'll meet your turn soon enough.

Joshua: — You don't understand... This city is finished... The crystal wall of those who believe in living like human beings instead of animals has crumbled... Don't you see? Don't you see what's happening to our city? Empathy is bankrupt, morality is collapsing, what's left are our individualities in the form of narcissistic collectivity... Just look closely, you will see that selfishness has become the law of accelerated beings. No one has patience anymore, it's just cursing instead of arguing... Just want the shit to be solved by any means to then return to their pathetic unrealities. Nobody lynches someone without first thinking of himself instead of the collective, this communitarianism shit is pure hypocritical bullshit... Everything here is just business... Business between individualists who want to live in peace. That's how we live in Tech City.

Charlie: — Invading people's privacy... Their thought is business?

Joshua: — You don't remember how it started, do you? Before it was just behavioral data, where you clicked, accessed, how long you accessed, your decisions. Algorithms with artificial intelligence to measure reactions, metaphysical insights of data from analysts to reach a perfect behavior of society... When they realized that all that shit was worthless... and was driving the financial market, corporate stocks and what was left of community stocks to collapse... it was too late.

Joshua gave a laugh and continued: — We've created a behavior with no turning back... You can't go back and say that all this garbage was a fluke stop... a temporary thing... No, man. I can't... We were the ones who created this shit in the belief that we could base performance data on people's reactions... But deep down... we ourselves were building those reactions in an artificial way, inflating the whole fucking thing to the point of imploding... making us what we are today.

Charlie: — And you with your futuristic ideology, you come in putting the stick on the table, giving a solution to the corporations.

Joshua: — Someone has to give them what they want... Feed this addiction to illusory power over people.

Charlie: — Fuck Joshua... It's the fucking thoughts... People's thoughts... What is in their unconscious ... You don't think they crossed the line, do you?

Joshua: — People today don't even know what they want. Everything comes ready... Just put some lights, some cool stuff and they buy... A little anger here, hate there and everything is perfect... They're just software that comes with the hate code built in. So it makes the whole thing easier. What was going on with the data wasn't working anymore. Who do you think is funding all this shit? Yes... Everybody, man. Everybody. No one gets left behind. Every time... Every penny... Every attention... It's all payment for more... The attention addiction... Now you understand... The corruption is in the data itself... and what they make us do for them.

Charlie: — Not so different from you... A will to change tainted by the filth of hypocrisy... Exploiting people's thinking.

Joshua: — You are very innocent...

Charlie: — What do you mean?

Joshua: — Neurodatta is everything man... Everything... It existed before you existed... It was discovered as a binary magnetic flux within the continuous layers of the quantum data field... We just replicated it in people...

Charlie: — What do you mean. Did they already exist?

Joshua: — Neurodatta can be what we are doing now, something that transcends cause and effect. You may be inside

Neurodatta and not know it, or worse, your behavior may just be a programmed structure inside Neurodatta... Being merely the replication of the determination of the data...

Charlie: — Are you telling me that there is a parallel reality to mine that controls what I do?

Joshua: — No. We are the parallel reality itself in reality... We are walking in the middle ground between fate and choice... Data circulates in our cybernetics and we don't know if something happens because we want it to or not.

Charlie: — So who controls all this shit?

Joshua: — You may just be unconsciously being manipulated into doing what you do.

Charlie removed the cigarette from his mouth and put the pistol against Joshua's face: — You mean a shot in your face will be involuntary? Fucking talk... Who's controlling us?

Joshua gave a sarcastic laugh: — Do you know that phrase? Forgive them for they know not what they do? It suits our situation very well... It might as well be... Forgive them for not knowing why they do what they do.

Lucy reading the duplicate and extracted data, spoke up: — Easy there, Charlie. He makes it difficult for us here.

Joshua: — Or is this all just a new form of Texture?

Lucy: — Don't listen to him... He just wants to mess with your head.

Joshua: — You haven't understood... Everything is information; we are just part of a small code of this whole sea of information... The binary codes transform our reality, all thoughts, all wills, all senses... We replicate in the neuro- cybernetic layers and integrate information... This shit is all binary... Everything is binary... So we are binary ... Yes or no... right or wrong... ally or foe... Kill or be killed... Feeding the Manichean desire behind every Machiavellian subject... The codes change shape and mutate all the time. So we can't create a perfect location within Neurodatta... Only breaks... But that's already necessary for us to be able to reassure society.

Charlie: — Why are you telling me this?

Joshua: — I have nothing left to lose... Soon my data will be duplicated... I will become disposable to Cybermind.

Lucy: — Don't listen to him Charlie.

Joshua smiled wryly: — That's the basis of Neurodatta... Connecting to the cybernetic structure to modify people's unconscious...

Charlie: — Are you telling me that this is the big breakthrough of our age? The ball of the crop? You guys? All right then...

Joshua: — No... You don't understand... Don't tell me you're the most sensible guy in town you're not Charlie... A fucking cyber-terrorist who suffered some shit like that with Neurodatta... She's trying to tell you something. You wired your unconscious directly to accidentally collide with her... I think that's why we're here... She wants to tell you something... I don't know what it is. She's always existed. It's a living organism of information that wanders in our unconscious to conduct our lives...

Charlie: — You guys changing this... You think you're gods?

Joshua: — This has nothing to do with being God... But with

control... Cybermind partners with major governments... The signs are in the streets and side conversations are the best source of voting influence... It's all about power.

Charlie then spoke indignantly: — You could change everything, man... This whole rotten system built by corporations... that sucked every last drop of hope out of this city... I saw them feed ignorance to facilitate the manipulation of good, honest people who became increasingly ignorant, sunk under the excesses of virtualized spectacles, turned into digital zombies, addicted to one more look, something that took over all their lives... I saw them steal every minute, every precious time, and every penny from those eager for novelty, everyone who put their money into an intangible virtuality, and something that comforted the pain of people who became more and more lonely, trapped in their individuality in the digital world... I saw the land of the peasants, workers with fertile land that was destroyed to build factories for components and enhancements... The problem is that in this society there are few good people in a world full of assholes... Now... Now there's no turning back from this shit, is there? Progress has turned us into animals... What was is gone now... The desires of novelty have influenced the way of seeing things... In the end, everything changed, with the false taste of free will... People wanted it that way and so it was done through their alienated wills in cyberspace... The fuck knows that violence is good for this absolute system, so it feeds the corporations even more... They overthrew necrocapitalism to live in a blood narcissistic naturalness... Just look at the newspapers... Cybernetic implants grow by record margins every year while people are starving... This is the dream world. The place where you stop eating to have the parade of the moment...

Charlie glared angrily at Joshua and continued: — You're a fucking psychopath... Guys like you are the ones who have left all of this in irreparable shit. You're just another son of a bitch with no comeback.

Joshua: — And you have back? Look at you... With dark

circles from attention fatigue in cyberspace, euphoric cybernetics in broken bodies... The codes have left you driven to ignorance and savagery. Living in the improvisation of stupidity in the form of hypocritical humanism.... You think you're free of yourselves and masters of the world But you are only transparent puppets of binarisms penetrated in your biological structures... You're nothing but Manichean tools in a game of virtual algorithms directing your reactions? You asked for this... You asked for this life. We're on the same side. The difference is I'm a builder and a nurturer of it all. I'm just a predetermined fucking avant-garde response.

Charlie looking to the side, swallowed and released the smoke: — No man... You're no vanguardist. You're just another who is part of this failed system, which tries to hang to not fall from what was left of the tower of Babel. A survivor who earns at the expense of others' suffering, exploiting their wills and vulnerabilities.

As the twinkle in Joshua's eyes faded and his expression turned serious. Charlie continued: — I'm just a data hijacker, cloud thief... I just want to fuck up the whole fucking... The whole fucking thing that people like you helped build. No... You're wrong. We're not on the same side.

Lucy then said to Charlie: — It happened. I got it.

Charlie then pointed the pistol at Joshua's head and spoke: — Everyone bowed to the implants... Suck the badass... The builder of our evolution. Now you're the man. The most avant-garde of junk.

A flash in the shed. Single shot to Joshua's forehead that went out right there... Charlie and Lucy were seen walking through the holes in the wall by the revolving machine guns, their footsteps echoing in the trail of bodies of the Foxyes killed by Cybermind at the entrance... Soon, the Cybermind guards in a trail of death from the stairs to the exit of the shed, ending with Joshua dead sitting on the table with his head to the side having a hole in his forehead dripping blood.

Nothing special. It was just another ordinary day in Tech City. Blood and deaths in dream form under the lights reflected in the faces of those excitedly experiencing the future. Charlie and Lucy leaving the shed saw shot cars that were turned into paper by bullets, on fire with torn bodies ahead... The four dead guys... All left on the dreamy fringe of living in Tech City.

***

In the car as Lucy drove to the meeting with Franklin.

Charlie asked: — I wonder if what he said is true.

Lucy: — From what?

Charlie: — Of being part of that unconscious system.

Lucy: — I really don't know.

Charlie: — What if it is? What's left of us?

Lucy: — And if the whole city goes? What's left of all of us?

Charlie: — So we're just part of a grand scheme... A system much bigger than we can imagine... Damn it... They've totally crossed the line... They're fucking with people's heads all over the place.

Lucy: — So you're saying you're a hero?

Charlie: — I just want to survive... To stop being controlled by this system that makes people think what they don't want to think.

Lucy: — It's too much power... I wonder what they must have done already... Workers, students, religious, corporations, hackers, assassins, mercenaries and even the politicians of this city.

Charlie: — It's animals controlling animals... In a cybernetically humanized park... Spectators manipulated by what they don't know why they believe.

Lucy: — You know... Sometimes I think that maybe it would have been better to have died in that accident than to know all this.

Charlie: — I also think... But we don't know if what Joshua said is real or not.

Lucy: — What we know is that we have to go to Cybermind.

Charlie: — Or were we programmed to go there?

Lucy: — What if destiny didn't exist? We can build our own destiny.

— What if the construction is not just part of an alternate path of one's own destiny? So we are cogs in a collective unconsciousness.

— Just another binary behavior among a million codes. Part of a system in constant maintenance.

She then tapped the pistol at her waist twice with her fingernail: — Here's the tool.

Charlie with melancholic eyes thinking about everything that was said. He calmly shared with Lucy: — Did you stop to think that this thing of not letting us go... Be...

Lucy's voice then became soft: — A destiny? I thought... We

were fated to be together.

— Maybe this is a dead end... One last reminder of something good before I die in this town.

— I don't want to. I don't want to be away from you... You're the best thing that ever happened to me in all this chaos.

— I don't know what to do if we stay away from each other. Would it be aches and pains of longing? I feel that thinking like this is better To have a romantic lucidity in the midst of it all.

— This should be our love story. Two people alone in the world, left at the mercy of society who found themselves in a data theft job.

— This is our real story... The reality of two people who are dying and started to like each other when things got complicated.

— It could be that the emotions that happened are the cause... The explanation for everything we're feeling right now... I don't know what it is... I just know I don't want to be away from you.

— It could be what we've been running from... Where we put all that hate... The anger lost in the lonely eyes.

— Or maybe we are the key... The answer to our problems... Something so in our faces that even we can't see it ourselves.

— You know, I... I've thought a lot about what you said... That thing that haunts you.

A tear came out of Lucy's eye and she quickly wiped it away and continued with her hands on the steering wheel: — From dreams?

— I don't believe... Or don't want to believe... Is this

unconscious force talking to us?

Lucy: — I wonder if it's not her? My mother?

— Maybe she really could be helping us.

— Yeah... Maybe that's her.

— Could it be that this force is uniting us more and more?

— It could be... Because I feel more connected to you. I feel at ease, a different feeling, like I'm already home.

— Tech City is our home. But it is we who are our home.

Then he followed the car down the road. Brake lights, three continuous horizontal neon lights from side to side of the rear following onwards under the road reflected with the lights of the lampposts... Darkness took over, until the continuous lights were dimming, forming a bright red line in the night background... Far away and above the darkness of the road... Lights, advertisements on top of the buildings, square illuminations of the apartments.... It was back the sound of engine with passage of something, they were not voices, but things and city sounds marking the presence in a busy place. The high dark buildings highlighted the neon's climbing the city, only the indirect lights from bottom to top, like a show, having as the only stage the frenetic spectacle of the performance taken in an active society without fear of tomorrow.

GHOST

Franklin: — I managed to disrupt the system... The codes we got from Joshua will do the trick. After I disable thecameras, we won't have much time to get in.

Lucy: — Thank you Franklin.

Charlie: — Do you know this could be a dead end?

Franklin: - We'll manage... We'll get out of this.

Cameras were being transmitted with repeated scenes in the security room and door sensors turned off. The garage gate opened and came an electromagnetic pulse disc splitting into a few parts, looking for the targets in the parking lot, were discs circling until reaching the guards... Isolated screams were heard, lonely echoes scattered in several parts as Charlie, Lucy and Franklin passed through the garage gate that came down closing itself little by little.

Entering and seeing the guards on the ground unconscious, the steps were fast, sneaky and with the machine guns pointed down. Charlie braced the cars, Franklin in the pillars and Lucy always in the cars opposite to those that Charlie was... They took turns on the sides, crossing the sides all the time to watch each other's backs.

Those white lights with blue on the ceiling drew glittering lines on the chrome details of the cars, highlighting the metallic paintings. The reflection of the ceiling in the middle term made itself follow the atmosphere of loneliness amidst the steps and pauses going towards the emergency staircase.

Franklin locked the garage door and left extra disks near the elevator in case any surprises occurred and they were caught from behind. Metal popping noise of the emergency door opening, which then lightly slammed the steel echoing in the silence of the garage.

Always looking up with the machine gun watching

everything at all times as they climbed the stairs. Sounds of the scraping of the soles of careful steps in a pure silence to the top of the building.

Franklin speaking into the radio: — According to Joshua's system it's on the twenty-eighth floor. The board is next to the Official Test System.

Charlie: — Tests where? In people's minds?

Halfway up they heard a noise of the door opening, leaning on the corner of the staircase walls... Two guards opened the door to the twelfth floor and went up... The echo of their footsteps harmonized the expressions of their voices during the ascent in a matter of corridors among the staff.

Right guard: — I don't know, man. I think this is probably just a legend... You guys make up a lot of stories.

Left guard: — I'm telling you the truth, man. It's a ghost, yeah.

— Isn't it a spy? Or some virus implanted in the central system?

— What virus is going to open a guy in the middle?

— Yeah. I think you might be right...

And right on the emergency stairs, on the fifteenth floor there was an exit that led to the window, a balcony in the middle of the stairs. A place for smokers... The guards paused at that moment to smoke and continue the conversation. Still confused... As much as their objectives were other, the three downstairs went up slowly to understand better the subject.

The guard on the right lit a cigarette: — But I can't believe it...

Suddenly the bodies of the guys appeared.

Sound of the machine gun being set up, it was the guard on the left pointing the cigarette down while the guard on the right lit the cigarette in his mouth with a lighter... After taking a drag the guy on the left answered: — I'm telling you. There is some nocturnal ghost here in the company.

— And why doesn't this ghost get out of here?

— He wants something from us.

— Shut the fuck up. We'd all be dead if I wanted to.

— Then answer me why are we seeing bodies every day in here?

— I don't know.

— Ghost man...

— A murderous ghost that came here to kill everyone and won't leave... If the people who can't stand it want to get out of this shit... Why wouldn't he? I'm more worried about other things... Have you heard the stories that are going on upstairs on the 20th floor?

— I can't believe... Experimenting with human beings... Alives... I don't know if it's true.

— Now you're going to tell me you don't believe in what we hear around here, and you're going to believe in ghost stories? Huh.

— It's bizarre stuff, man... A company doing this to people... It's impossible to believe... Macabre.

— I can't wait to get my hands on some hard cash and get the hell out of here...

— You love to put batteries in, don't you? Come on. You gonna be afraid of a ghost?

— I'm afraid I'll be the next experiment.

— Deep down... I think we're already the experience... Experience of that ghost.

— They wouldn't be stupid enough to kill their own security guards.

— After that story that they were taking the guys from the asylum to test implants in schizophrenics to see how far the reality and insanity of the human being would go... I don't expect anything else.

— Really... The guys did this parade... I still can't believe it.

— Fred was witness to an experiment... They removed the guy's neural implant and fabricated a parallel reality where he believed there was no death and no danger... turning him into a fearless soldier.

— I wonder who they sell this stuff to?

— Governments... Those who can't handle too much information go crazy... They get help from the government to get hospitalized... and from there... the craziest ones come here to become an experiment... I don't know... That's my theory.

— You take off and come back a soldier without a homeland...

— The guys ended up creating a Cyberproxy war... I prefer to say Crazyproxy... Proxy warfare of backless madmen turned painless soldiers.

— Why don't they cure the guys? They don't treat them? If they've already know.

— Because it's not profitable, man. You still haven't learned how things work around here.

Soon the soldiers heard someone on the radio saying "*Everyone on alert... Body found on the seventeenth floor*". The guard on the right threw the cigarette on the ground and stepped on it, crushing it with the tip of his right foot. Just as one could see the left guard throwing the cigarette away, near the space with flowers near the window and continued the subject: — The ghost has just attacked.

— You come in here with that ghost stuff...

Going towards the door as they opened the voices were distant with the conversation... The guard on the left answered: — It's true man... It's a ghost.

— Careful, man... Soon you go crazy and end up here being experience to become a soldier without emotion.

Smiling ironically he replied: — Come on man... Shut your mouth.

The door closed, Charlie, Lucy, and Franklin looked at each other, not understanding that conversation... No one would say what was going on so naturally.

Charlie then spoke up: — I think we should take a look.

Lucy: — There is something strange going on here.

Franklin: — Whatever it is... You're fucking with these guys.

Charlie: — Fuck with them... It's good for us.

Lucy: — I don't know if it's a good thing to go.

Charlie gives a smile the side of his mouth: — Come on.

Entering the emergency door on the seventeenth floor they came across desks divided by office partitions... Computers blacked out... Everything was totally dark. Office corridor, seeming to be the accounting floor, containing several papers on tables, computers and a standardized organization. Leaving a strange climate that made me realize those partitions where each one worked in a quiet way... Even in that silence it was possible to feel and to imagine the sounds of the phones ringing, keyboards beating, papers being moved and low parallel conversations... A typical office.

It was very dark and the lights wouldn't come on. The only way to see was through the flashlights of the weapons, because it seemed that every cybernetic system was turned off and corrupted on that floor, the night visions of the ocular systems didn't work... Not even the simplest of implants. The bodies seemed a bit heavy, and in that climate one could see the total vulnerability of the three of them facing a dark corridor with only the light of the lanterns to help.

Charlie looked up, put the flashlight in a place near the lamp on the ceiling and said on the radio: — Shit... Look here.

Lucy: — Fivetech... Power destabilizers.

Franklin: — Nothing will help here. We'll only have the bullets to help.

The lanterns circled the desks and partitions of the office, the weather said not to be alarmed, it was to keep walking sneakily to the end of the corridor. That's when they saw that guard walking slowly, trembling with pain, his arms half open to the sides, moaning and

with a bloody uniform... He groaned as he walked... It was pain... No one knew where... Until he spoke with his voice trembling with pain:
- Please. Get out... You will die.

His body slowly lost strength until he fell to the ground. As they approached the hallway they heard cries of pain coming from the hallway at the end of the office *"Ah!"*. Noise of steel hitting. *"Ah!!!!"*. Machine gun fire. Noise of steel being torn apart. *"Ah!"*. Gunfire. And several screams of pain with the sound of flesh being cut. *"Ah!"*. *"Ah!"*. *"Ah!"*. The flashlights pointed upwards, followed by that sound of death with flesh being cut, body falling to the ground, along with the sound of plastic and uncontrolled lights swinging on the ground. It was when Charlie, Lucy, and Franklin reached the entrance to this hallway and saw the guard crawling around bathed in blood who spoke: — It's the devil. It's the devil. We're all dead.

When they reached the corridor the circles of the lanterns and the uncontrolled fluorescent lamps with failing lights exposed all the bodies in that half-dark atmosphere All keeping them dead. Some sitting on the wall with a trail of blood above, others on the floor with blood splattered on the ceiling and a puddle on the floor. One even tried to run and could see his body to the side and legs torn off at the other end of the hallway and holes in his back. Another was seen hanging from the wall with the rifle slung across his chest, through until it wedged into the wall. Some weapons destroyed. One could see some fingers moving from the reflexes of the nerves of recent death, the smell was hot from the open bodies sharing the same moment of terror.

The circles of the lanterns and the failing lights evidenced the horror of that corridor... Highlighting the faces cut by the sides of the mouth, lacerations of bodies and exposed flesh with sparks. A crazy arrived to lose the plug of the forehead in a precise cut, died seated leaning on the wall of the corridor, scared of open eyes, open mouth and a part of the brain exposed, his plug was in the ground while sparks came out around the brain cut in half. Corridor of blood from the hands on the walls. One could see clearly the broken of beaten to the side with the body on the floor with the head sunk in. While reading at the end of the corridor the words written in blood *"Ghost"*.

Blood trails from the footsteps of the three advanced to the end of the hallway and they saw a dented battered door with blood in the middle, followed by the body of the guard on the floor. As they entered the room they saw their cybernetics returning and more failed lights from neon fluorescent bulbs... The pantry with several huge boxes, looking like a small shed. As they entered they came across guards at the end of that aisle of boxes facing the flashing light with their backs to them. They were going after this ghost... Hidden on the corners of the boxes the three saw the two guards pointing their guns at the end of the corridor... Soon, one could see that thin light passing by and a shout into the first guard. *"Uhf!!!"*. Meanwhile, the second guard looked at him and that guy with his hands on his stomach kneeling in pain that slowly faded away, slowly falling forward.

Frightened he shot to the side: — Come out you son of a bitch... Are you scared?

A light behind him hitting the back of his leg caused him to turn the light of the flashlight back into the hallway, machine gunning the walls he continued: — Come on... Come out.

At this moment Charlie looked out of the corner of his eyes and saw approaching from the back of the boxes the footsteps. A flashlight behind the guard, ripping his head off and hitting the side of the box hard, splashing uncontrolled blood from his head into the air that fell to the ground rolling. The body fell to the side with the impact of the cut and another lantern light on the floor showing another death on the ghost's account.

It was kind of quiet... Nobody knew anything anymore...

what it was and where it was... They were approaching little by little ... When the three of them arrived at the end of the corridor they found two other doors, they chose to enter in the one that was stained with blood. It led to a luxurious room with an office coffee table with two more doors on the sides and a glass one that opened to the sides... Soon, the three of them made their way to that door that led to a wide open balcony... It had a beautiful view of the city, you could hear the sound of cars and noise of the city in motion and the lights on the horizon amid the buildings ... On top of the thick acrylic wall was that person, the ghost, with metallic and leather clothes, crossing the implants. The legs, arms and face with lines and traces of implants and a dark green scarf swinging back on the neck. The ghost was in full balance, sitting with both legs lying on top of the wall, right knee bent upwards, propping one hand on the ground behind his back and his right arm propped on the knee of the raised leg... Looking at the horizon with the samurai sword on his back that reflected its chrome in the darkness. It was her... Who looked away and said: — I've been waiting for you.

Soon Charlie put the machine gun down and said: — Jeniffer?

NEURODATTA

Jeniffer climbed down from the wall as they approached and stood right there on the edge of the balcony while she spoke: — They brought me... They performed some modifications that made me recover very quickly that very day that they broke into Dylan's apartment. They were little robots that altered my entire body. They modified some parts and other parts they couldn't change.

Charlie's eyes filled with tears: — You didn't tell me you had the armor on I thought you were dead.

Jeniffer: — They saved me.

Lucy: — How did you escape?

Jeniffer: - Dylan. Figuring it might occur that they might find us he put an Electronic Metamagnetism Reformulator (REM) on me that disabled their devices. Just as he also gave me a Fivetech Rebootcrack that destabilizes a small power grid. Like the one I used on that floor. When I became aware of everything and all things started to make sense, they would shut down my mind, it was at this point that I recovered with the modifications they made to me They thought the sword was mine, and put a modification with abilities to use it.

Lucy: — Did they give you skills?

Charlie: — They were building another soulless soldier...

Jeniffer: — They have a system that can increase abilities that are already conditioned.... If the person already has propensities for certain abilities, an oversizing of them happens... A system that I did not know existed, capable of stretching all the psychocorporal factors connected in the middle between the electrochemical neuroconnections and the nanocapacitances of the cyberhub, mixing the bits with the superconditionings of learning, looking like a kind of metabolic function of neuroplasticity... In the end it all worked out... But sometimes...

Charlie: — What?

Jeniffer: — Sometimes I get deep headaches... I feel someone different inside me... Like another personality... I don't know...

Lucy: — Something we need to worry about? Jeniffer: - No... I don't think so.

Franklin: — If they gave your abilities. Why did you kill them?

Jeniffer: — It's not that simple. I'm on Geospectrometer Inversion Dialer (GID) which causes me to weaken when I get close to them, my systems start crashing and the weird thing is the more I go up the floors. The weaker I get. And the worst happens also when I try to leave the building.

Franklin: — You haven't finished the process... So you're wired into their system. It may be an emergency measure so that none of their experiments can get out of the building, much less rebel.

Jeniffer: — I've been waiting for you ever since. Hoping that you could come to Cybermind... I believed you wouldn't let them get away with what happened... I knew you were alive the day Isabelle called, she had just woken up. I saw them on the screen.

Charlie: — I wouldn't leave you with them.

Jeniffer: — I wanted to come up with you guys. But I can't... I could die if I go up there... That's the main room.

Charlie: — We get to know about the room.

Jeniffer: — I don't know what to do... I'm stuck here in this building.

Lucy: — I can take a look at what they did to your system. I don't know if I'll be able to reverse it.

Lucy then plugged her top wire from her wrist into the back of Jeniffer's neck... Jeniffer's eyes lit up and turned purple. Lucy's turned pink... Without plugging anything in Franklin's eyes turned green and he spoke: — Ok Lucy... Now give me access to your biodisk.

Franklin continued: — I'm in. Lucy: - It's a cryptic mess in here.

Franklin: — Looks like the same sequence. Identical to your sequence. Where it reconfigures itself all the time and transforms procedurally into new combinations of disk.

Charlie: — And what does that mean?

Lucy: — She is in the same boat as us.

Franklin: — Only by getting clearance directly from the central system to reverse.

Jeniffer: — So you mean I have to stay here? If you die... Will I be here forever?

Franklin: — There's no way. You'll have to wait for us... Take this here... This chip is my chipdisk, plug it into the back of my head, we'll have a modular recap intranet connection, so when I plug it in, you'll be on the network along with it and we'll be able to reverse this cryptographic connection, resetting the DIG settings... Same setup goes for both of you... Now that she is involved I think it is better that you also get those chipdisks so we can connect directly... Before, we didn't need to because we were going to connect directly. Chipdisks are good too. It'll take longer to process, but it'll do the trick.

The three of them took the chipdisks, plugged them into the back of their heads and Charlie spoke: — All right.

Jeniffer: — You can come up... I'll take care of the guards downstairs; I won't let anyone come up.

***

On the twenty-eighth floor the initial door was a glass door that opened... Which was easy to enter with all the codes extracted from Joshua.... As they entered the white lights on the ceiling came on. A large hall with white floors glowing to the point of reflecting the room, containing a few other glass doors around the corners with light blue LEDs on their sides, tables with transparent computers in a hallway to the end of the room that led to another clear glass double door behind a central table at the end of the hallway. The table with the front of the base in light blue led and   the door at the end of the room in its right side with light blue led also. A combination of light colors that stood out in the clean room.

When they entered the glass door they saw an open place with several corridors of screens, open with yellow handrails on both sides, just like the ones built in factories, metal corridors making a hexagonal turn with five floors followed by metal stairs below that led to the core of that place which had something important to reveal. Around white goo followed by several wires around it.... Men covered up to the top of their heads with hoods and overalls coated in a special white plastic material. They were working without caring what was around them, some were messing with the transparent computers and others had a transparent device in their hands during their analysis surrounding that white goo... More of them were checking the wires and you could see others talking to each other looking at the mobile devices   standing   around discussing something while you could see the hot fumes from the coffees under the table.

Seeing all that, the three walked in that dark, their steps directed to the right staircase made slight noise on that metallic floor... They could only see the central white light amidst the metal and railings between the floors. On that same floor, without noticing in the dark, they saw that woman with a white coat and a pistol on her right hand looking to nothing. Her face and her coat reflected little by little as the white goo shone strongly on the floors below. Not understanding anything, they were getting closer... The white lights of the goo reflected more his face, eyes and the coat... Yes... She was there... Isabelle.

Isabelle: — You still don't understand, do you? Lucy: - Isabelle is gone... End of the line.

— We're on the same side.

Charlie: — No one is on your side... It's gone... Joshua's dead... You're all alone...

— You people are so innocent... You can barely see what's

really going on.

Franklin: — We know who's to blame for all this. That's enough.

Charlie: — How can you? All these people? You're reading their thoughts... Changing them.

Isabelle: — That's not the point.

Charlie: — And what the fuck is the point?

— Everything is ready... No one can control themselves anymore... Cybernetic irrationality has taken over this city. We're all numb right now. You don't remember what it was like before. It started with simple polarization of ideas, tribalized lives, high rates of Manichean behavior, people were forced to commit suicide simply because they weren't part of the systemic... They weren't good enough for any idea, you either joined an idea or you were attacked from both sides, mentally and physically... It was total chaos... The war was just a trigger for something irreversible. We became binary savages in a coded jungle. I found our solution. The solution to our problem... Anesthesia.

Charlie: — Do you think you know people? Do you think you know them enough to want to control them? The truth is you don't know anything about them.

Isabelle: — After everything I've learned... After everything I've seen... I can tell you that... I know one thing... People are afraid of dying, but not afraid of killing...

Charlie: — You're just justifying an excuse to say you're reading people's thoughts.

— They can't go back to the way it was... Even with this shit out of control... You think nothing can get worse? Robbery and homicide rates are extremely high in Tech City. You're part of it. These aren't system failures, or even hits, they're just reactions derived from freedom without anaesthesia, thoughts outside of themselves. Decentralization is tempting, but it is a utopia with many consequences.... And they answer my question rhetorically... How many people did you kill to get here?

Charlie: — You don't understand... People deserve to think on their own, without anyone knowing, without anyone interfering. Where's the free will? The will of their own? The private desire? We killed because we had to... We had to get this far... You have to stop this, Isabelle.

Isabelle: — The old excuse... Killing because you had to... It was necessary to fulfill your will to survive... Who's being hypocritical here?

Charlie: — If we die... Who's gonna stop you from doing this shit?

Isabelle: — It seems that the means really do justify the ends... Everything indicates that we are on the same side... You still don't understand.

Lucy: — Charlie... I think only a bullet can solve this bitch's problem.

Isabelle: — If I die... The whole town dies.

Lucy: — Does the whole town die?

Isabelle: — I am interconnected with the entire cognitive system of the city... In an obtuse cloud... I do not read their thoughts on me that would be too much... Their minds are only connected to my life force.

Franklin: — You call that freedom? You call that free will?

Isabelle: — I call it an insurance policy against people like you.

Lucy then pointed the machine gun at Isabelle and spoke: — Then so be it.

— You wanna pay to see? I'm ready to die... But I want to know if you are too... Charlie is too?

Charlie: — Lucy... Put that shit down.

Lucy: — This bitch can't go unpunished... We have to put an end to her race.

—I put a damper on people... I know what they talk... What they think... But at the same time I don't know... If that's what they're worried about... That's the future... Anesthesia.

Charlie: — Okay... Since you say you're doing good for this town... Tell me... What about the data you sell to corporations? Were you doing humanity a favor with an office inside WeaponTech?

— We see only reflections of thoughts... What's exposed still takes work... We have a solid partnership with WeaponTech... We provide the data and they give us the technology to better read the neural information... Afair trade. Don't you think? The problem was that pulse that kept them from Neurodatta... And somehow they managed to neutralize the location of your friend here... I don't know how... We can find anyone... Even those who have neuroproxy and believe they live hidden from cybernet... If it wasn't for that pulse, we would have found you by now.

Isabelle took a cigarette, lit it and continued: — But this week everything was ready... We are putting into practice the universal code that we can totally decipher thought... To connect totally with the unconscious to the point of being able to produce it... There was still a black hole hiding some obscure data from the unconscious... I don't know what it was. Everything was ready, we would have total access and we could put all this information on a simple chipdisk... Until Jones opened his mouth.

Isabelle took a drag and spoke: — He knew everything that was going on... We were going to elect him, kind of tight so as not to arouse suspicion... But he betrayed us.

Charlie: — You're telling me he was part of all this shit?

— He knew in parts... When he found out everything and what we were just finishing up... Then he snapped like anyone who doesn't understand the whole thing.

Lucy: — You fucking bitch... You got him into this and then you discarded him like he was nothing.

Isabelle took another drag on her cigarette and spoke: — Welcome to Tech City politics... That's the way things work around here.

Charlie: — And what are you going to do when you deploy this universal shit?

Isabelle looked down showing the people working downstairs and said: — Don't you see my newest prototype? Great workers... They don't complain, they don't get tired, thoughtful, integrated into a single unconscious structure...

Lucy seeing that felt... Imagining her mother locked in a consciousness, it was the edges of feelings that filled to the core of her emotions... An eternal prison of data holding a thought, caging a soul and holding a spirit.... Someone impossible to break free... Her eyes widened, her breathing quickened, making her finger speak with the forward thrust of her hand... Firing the machine gun.

Isabelle's eyes glowed in a red light in anticipation of some reaction. Just as Lucy was firing, Isabelle leapt from above throwing the pistol to the side with only one hand as she jumped. Several shots that caught the three of them by surprise... It ended up grazing Franklin's belly and Charlie's right shoulder and another bullet that grazed Lucy's right leg.... The employees who had been working spontaneously grabbed their rifles and began firing from below. The bullets ricocheted, came up, sparks flew off the metallic floor hit by the bullets.

Charlie stood up quickly after being shot by Isabelle. Lucy limped a little, but held on while Franklin ran with his hand on his stomach. The three of them ran down the stairs until they could brace themselves against some metal boxes that blocked the frantic bullets fired by the guys downstairs.

Charlie spoke: — Fuck. She's really fast... She got ahead of Lucy.

Lucy: — How did she manage to catch us?

Franklin: — He shot without looking at us... Holy shit... Shoot her in the legs... So we can reverse her unconscious connection.

Charlie, even with his shoulder problems, managed to brace the machine gun... exchanging fire... Until hitting one of the guys, piercing his white jumpsuit, staining red in the marks of the bullets in his chest. At this moment Lucy saw the two shooting at him from the right corner, it was easy... Her eyes zoomed in and she managed to find a way to shoot propped up on the box, between the holes in the metal floor screen. The two guys simply raised their arms in surprise from the bullets hitting their chests, falling and disappearing into the darkness. Franklin then spoke up: — Cover me, I'm going to jump to get the guys who are on the computer down here I'll have my back to the others.

Machine guns rumbled, bullets popped, and the thin sound of piping bullets hitting metal. Lucy stood up a little to shoot at the same moment Charlie pulled to the side of the box firing down below and shouting to Franklin. *"Go! Go! Go!"*.

Franklin took off running and jumped the railing, falling one floor short and already rolled, where exactly the guys shot and the bullets almost hit him, leaning on the nearby table, hit hard with his shoulder by the impact of the rolling and shot the two guys. Giving him time to roll forward and hide at the next tables. The strategy worked so well that the guys downstairs started shooting at him to the point of being vulnerable to Charlie and Lucy, who also jumped in shooting the guys   The blood splashed diagonally on the floor from the impact of the bullets that went through the white overalls. One of them didn't let go of the machine gun finger and kept shooting and hitting some cables connected to the central goo. Soon, the Neurodatta core, followed by some computers near the center... They started to get a strong short.

And without a second thought Franklin stood up and said: — This is the one right here.

Taking a cable from his wrist and applying it to his central system... His eyes turned green... Connecting to the others... Charlie's eyes turned blue and Lucy's turned pink, all the biodisks connected through the chipdisks.

They heard a laugh from the very dark part of the room... It was Isabelle's voice: — Assholes.

Charlie shot up where he heard the voice and Lucy turned on her night vision, seeing that red streak going up, and shouted: — It went up.

Charlie and Lucy started to run up the stairs, but they didn't know where the shots were coming from... Lucy was confused, as she could only see lines going up the floors and shots coming from all corners... Meanwhile the Neurodatta's core was becoming more and more vulnerable; sparks were coming out, flashes with some electrical noises and sometimes crackling sounds like gunshots. Scaring everyone in the room.

Franklin on the radio. *"Shoot her in the legs... And plug one of the chipdisks into the back of her head... Let's reverse this fucking thing.... I'm trying to decode the code combination... The* Suggestionizer *is speeding up the whole process. "*.

At this moment Lucy could see the lights and couldn't reach them properly... In a surprise way, without knowing where, she was shot in the right arm, being forced to drop the machine gun and grab the pistol with her left hand, hiding in the corners, trying to dodge the shots... Charlie seemed frozen near one of the boxes... As if he was processing something and didn't know what it was... Franklin looked up and saw that guy on the ground on his knees with his hands on the ground screaming.... It was Charlie in desperation in the middle of that exchange of gunfire. "Ahhh!!!" "Ahhh!!!".

Charlie: — Fuck... It's fucking hurting... What a pain... Holy shit... What a fucking pain.

Lucy exchanging shots with a cross-line that paused upstairs and fired, giving Lucy time to hide in the box near the stairs.... Soon she said: — Hold on Charlie... We're almost there.

Charlie: — Fuck... It won't work... You're too sick... Help me Lucy... Help me Lucy... Help me Franklin ... I'm gonna die... It hurts so much.

Charlie's eyes went out, his body softened.... His eyes shorted out... When a strong pulse reverberated throughout the room, resonating through the walls, followed by a strong pressure destroying some computers in the room and releasing more wires from the Neurodatta core... Making Lucy jump up, Franklin almost fly, being held by his cable stuck to the table. More sparks and more bursts from the core made the room light up. The red streak stopped and at this moment Lucy got up and with a lot of pain in her body went up the rest of the remaining floors... Trying to follow her, Charlie was dragging himself little by little trying to climb... Not withstanding the pressure... And they both heard Franklin on the radio. *"Fuck... You won't believe it... This pulse connected me directly to her... No need to plug the chipdisk into her. I think it will work... What the fuck is going on? I am connected to a lot of things... If it wasn't for the Suggestionizer, I would be fucked, this shit would have fried me, fuck, I was connected to the core"*.

Lucy answered on the radio. *"Just fucking go."*

Charlie walking dizzy and seeing things a little crooked and blurry... He spoke into the radio. *"Fuck... What the fuck is going on?"*

Arriving at the top floor Lucy saw no one... But when she looked into the clear room from which they were standing she was startled... Everything was destroyed... All the equipment short-circuited, sparks coming out, broken, lamps hanging, the chaos of the pulse had taken over that room... The lights flickered and she couldn't see anything coming back. Soon, a silhouette appeared from the flashing lights in the room. Someone on the other side of the glass door... Two holes pierced the crystal clear bed the glass The shots went beyond the door and hit Lucy's legs.

The door opened with... It was Isabelle... Behind her back could be seen sparks, fallen wires and shorted computers... Her eyes flashed red slightly as she walked in. Until her eyes returned to normal the moment she was calmly walking over to Lucy   Then Isabelle spoke up: — You don't understand.

Lucy: — Fuck... My legs... Go fuck yourself Isabelle... Finish this fucking thing... Get it over with... Finish the job.

— You don't understand anything... We are on the same side... You don't understand. We're all doomed in the dice. The data has consumed every last drop of our soul. We are lost in time believing in a non-existent future, this is the future. Don't you see? We have created a dependency on data. Our drug, the addiction to the space of thoughts taken from us... A regret of the past coupled with the hope of acceleration wanting everything to be solved by any means necessary, to this point...

Lucy: — To the point of fucking up?

— The point where we have no way out anymore. We create our collective unconsciousness, we form predetermined behaviors, we build excited anticipations and you can't fight what is part of yourself, what is you.

Lucy: — Are you just trying to fix it and bring in less data processing?

Isabelle: — Fucking hell. That's what I've been trying to tell you all this time... Anesthesia... Cybernetic anesthesia.

Lucy: — And where is the free will?

— He's been gone a long time... A long time ago... I wish it was different... It is not power, it is making sure that humanity stays alive and survives in peace by what it has built itself through its digital excitement... Everyone today is part of Neurodatta, they create each other's thoughts... Voluntary social reactions become defense mechanisms of this cybernetic system... As much as I don't interfere, they have already shaped a way to circumvent themselves and drive thoughts into themselves on their own... An independent unconscious intelligence... Autonomous of any programming...

Lucy: — Fuck... So nobody in this shit is free of this shit?

Isabelle: — So I ask you... About everything that motivates you... Everything you feel, have felt, do and have done... Do you believe in freedom or have you been convinced that it exists?

Lucy: — It can't be...

Isabelle pointed the pistol and started talking to herself: — Don't do this to her... Please, I beg you... She doesn't need to know about this... No one here needs to... She doesn't know what she wants... She doesn't know... She doesn't know.

Isabelle continued talking to herself: — Okay... No... Don't do that... I beg you... No... Please... No.

Isabelle lowered the gun, but ready to get up again and finish the job right there: — Lucy... We are on the same side... Understand... I want a more balanced society, more natural in its way of being... Free... That can have its own choices... But for that someone has to take over... Someone has to sacrifice themselves to keep the Anesthesia.... Understand me... Please... Stay with me... What do you want?

Lucy pointed the gun and said: — What do I want? I just want to kill the bitch that locked up my mother.

Isabelle shot Lucy's pistol to the point where the gun bounced away and continued: — Who locked your mother up?

Lucy: — You bitch... I know everything... You brought her here... You put her consciousness into Neurodatta so she can control everyone and serve as your puppet... What promise did you give? To bring me back to her? I'll talk to her... Didn't you know? I speak to her through dreams... It is the signs... The symbolic signs of dreams that direct the path I should follow... And I ended up seeing everything... everything that happened to her... through the dreams.

Isabelle: — No... This is impossible... Come with me... This society needs us... United, transforming again the civilization lost in time... Soon you will understand all this that happens to you... These surges in the middle of the night... These dreams.

Lucy: — I just want to kill whoever arrested her here... It was you... And you will die.

Isabelle looks into Lucy's eyes, answering with a firm and concise expression: — No... You don't understand, Lucy... There's no way... There's no way I could have arrested her here Lucy... I didn't imprison your mother's consciousness in Neurodatta... Because I am your mother.

A tear came out of Lucy's eye and she screamed: — *No!!! That's a lie!!!!*

Isabelle, still holding the pistol in her right hand, put her hands on her head, knelt down and spoke in a tone of desperation to herself You couldn't say... You couldn't say... Now how is she going to kill you? How will she put you out of your misery? This was the intention... Now she won't want to kill us.

Lucy confused and understanding something hidden: — Mom?

Isabelle: — Lucy... Get out of here... Escape from here.

Isabelle pointed the gun as Lucy stood up and propped herself up on the edge of the hallway, almost falling down there... Isabelle stood up and spoke: — What are you doing? No... She has to die... That's the only way you can die too.

Lucy: — Charlie!

From the right corner of the floor, near the stairs... Charlie pointed a pistol with his left hand at Isabelle. She's not going to go with you.

Lucy: — Mom? Why?

Isabelle pointed the pistol at her own temple and spoke: — You wouldn't understand... You wouldn't understand.

Soon Franklin was heard on the radio. "*I did it... I reversed everything... I fucking did it... I did it... Ahhh!!!! Ahhh!!!*".

When Franklin finished talking... He ended up having a short in his systems and blacked out at the moment of the reversal of the three systems... Reversing the systematic connections of Lucy, Charlie, Isabelle and Jeniffer.

Her gaze was one of doubts between truths and untruths... Lucy found herself inconsolable for a doubtful truth, even if it has a percentage of questioning... She still wanted to believe what she heard, to believe in her search, and began to take short steps forward and said: - Don't do that mom... Don't do that...

Isabelle then pointed her pistol at Lucy: — It's time... The time is coming...

Charlie: — Put that shit down...

Lucy: — No Charlie... No...

Isabelle: — It's time... They're calling... Can't you hear it? All these unconsciousnesses calling my name? They are callingme.

Lucy: — Mom?

At this moment Isabelle shot Lucy in the chest near her right arm and Charlie shot Isabelle twice in the chest... Lucy fell backwards, without having much time to think, Charlie threw himself and managed to hold Lucy.... He with bullet pierced shoulder holding Lucy with little strength in his arm due to the gunshot Charlie soon said: — I can't hold on.

The iron of the side that Charlie was leaning on began to bend and come loose. Until it broke and he almost fell. He was left holding only one hand on the metal floor and the other holding Lucy. He countered the pain; the permanence and determination made those fingers give their all   Making

Charlie say to Lucy: — I won't let go   We will die together.

Below Neurodatta's core was letting off sparks and making popping noises. Shots and sounds of short bursts below Lucy who said: — Charlie we are both going to die.

Charlie: — I will save you. You're not going to die.

Both were holding each other's hand, below the core sparking, prosthetics withering away... Both making that force that didn't move out of place, not even sway. Still and intact in a moment that only the eyes could tell... He looked at her and she looked at him... They were the unspoken words in an indecipherable space of eternal parting time... They knew...

Her hands were loosening slightly... Until she looked into Charlie's eyes and said: — I love you.

Without resisting... The fingers let go. Opening up for the last touch of love before her eyes as she fell directly into Neurodatta's core... With half of her body dissolving into the information and the upper torso falling the other way after crossing the Neurodatta... Yes... It happened... And Charlie said: — Goodbye Lucy... I love you.

Without resisting with the other hand... He knew... Now it would be his turn... He even imagined that he would be very lucky to fall; fall on Neurodatta; and both of them will live forever in the data... In their purest cybernetic romance...

The fingers were loosening... He couldn't resist... He knew... He was falling... As his fingers left the floor... A hand quickly grabbed his arm... It was her... Jeniffer: — I got you.

She was lifting him up... Until Charlie sat down on the floor and said: — I don't believe it... I don't believe it man... She was gone.

Jeniffer: — Where is Franklin? And Lucy?

Tears of farewell came out of Charlie's eyes: — She fell down there... Man... She died... What the fuck... Franklin is down at the computer, unconscious.

Jeniffer: — I'll get him... I'll be right back... Hold on...

Charlie stood up, with his arm sparking and some parts of it broken off. He walked downstairs little by little... Finding Jeniffer who spoke to him: — I was coming to get you.

Charlie: — I'm fine... I went down to get what was left of her.

Jeniffer with Franklin in her arms spoke up: - I think there is an emergency staircase on that floor.... It only opens from the inside... I think we can go down it...

Charlie: — Is it safe down there? Jeniffer: - I took care of that...

They were coming down the emergency staircase. It was clear that something had happened. The central corridors of the building had several floors with several dead soldiers in th e corridors. Some electrocuted by the electromagnetic pulse, others cut down by Jeniffer... What could be seen was something frightening... Many, many bodies in the open corridors that crossed between floors... From above you could see bodies lying on the floor and a lot of blood running through the floors... Prosthetics torn off, weapons destroyed, no other living beings besides the two, all shamelessly annihilated... No story to tell...

As they were leaving the building the Neurodatta core began to explode... Several explosions took place in the building that came to have some floors explode and catch fire at the end of the avenue...

They were surviving Neurodatta. Jeniffer carried Franklin already on his feet, who were limping with pain in his body. Just as Charlie carried the other part of Lucy's body between his arms.

***

The sound of rain drops hitting the living room window. Franklin's eyes were unfocused and his face flashed a pale blue through the computer screen... Engaged in a pile of codes being built, broken and fixed in the private determination that surrounded that room. Fingers pounded on keyboards with thoughtful speed that demonstrated the stares fixed in high reflection under the atmosphere of concern.

Walking up to him came Charlie: — Hey there... How are you doing there?

Franklin: — I think we can make it.

Jeniffer approached Franklin and spoke up: — What do you think?

Franklin: — It's okay...

Taking a break, Franklin picked up a piece of printed paper

from the table, turned his chair around, and handing the paper to Charlie he spoke: — Tell me if this is really it....

Charlie: — Holy shit. Is it really here?

Jeniffer: — Let me see... It could be... It could be...

Franklin: — I think it is... From the impression I got from the electrography... There is a lot of current going through there. And it seems to redistribute itself to feed its own power.

Soon Franklin took the transparent tablet and showed it to him: — See this dynamic of magnetic passage? It's going all the way to the core... I found this system when we connected to Isabelle...

Charlie: — It could be over there... I hope it is.

Jeniffer touched Charlie's shoulder and spoke: — Yes it is Charlie... Let's trust that it is... It's going to be alright...

Jeniffer: — So this is where the guys had been running the whole thing....

Charlie: — Cyberdatta. We have to go there.

Franklin: — It's not like that... There are many powerful people behind...

Jeniffer: — Then it's time to strike from above....

Charlie: — We were hiding from everyone... Now it's about time these sons of bitches got to know us... They will know who we really are ... In a way they've never seen before...

Charlie then changed his expression when he looked back... His concern was evident in all of this: — I hope we can make it.

Jeniffer answered: — We'll manage...

And right behind them was Lucy's body with wires connected to her body Some connected to the ceiling, some to computers, and some screens with various codes going around, looking for a way to reboot...

Franklin: — I don't think Neurodatta killed her...

Charlie: — What's your theory?

Franklin: — I think your consciousness has been transferred into Neurodatta... From what I'm seeing here... I don't think she died...

Charlie: — Why do you think so?

Franklin: — There is an obtuse code rapidly circulating on the net... It goes through and through the production engines and binary links.

Jeniffer: — That could be her.

Franklin's eyes widened when he looked at something different on the screen. It's her.

The computers suddenly began to blur the screens... The images were blurred as if they were defective... Franklin, frightened, said: — What the fuck is going on?

Noticing quick flashes through the window, the lights seemed to be flashing... But no, it was the problems on the screens all over the city... All the signs... All the computers... Charlie seeing all that through the window spoke up: — Look here...

All defective signs... Signs of remembrance... Signs of freedom... Signs of evolution... Signs of a message reflected in a collective absolute... It could be a madman who decided to turn the fuck on and hacked everything to show himself, trying to appear and say he is the coolest of the time... It could be a simple problem in Cybernet that would soon be fixed to keep paradise turned on in a desert of reality... Or they were messages from someone who ended up knowing the truth of the reality behind the illusions...

Flashing lights that interrupted the access of the devices... They were lights that stopped the city... Lights of an imperceptible path... Lights that made you wake up from deep dreams of unrealities...

Electronic defect colors with shades of freedom... A different freedom... Where the mind awoke to a new form of dream, something no one would be able to believe in... What would beliefs be without the lights? What would beliefs be without the attentions? If it was there... It was then... It happened... No one will believe it...

The glow of the lights flashed... Reflected in their faces... Charlie, Jeniffer and Franklin felt the luminous madness, watching standing by that window all the city lights flashing...

Of all the people in the city... Only they knew Only they realized... That it was her... Lucy...

Seeing all that... They saw... What could be starting? No one knew what it was... But the truth was there... Told by someone who had seen the cybernetic society from the inside...

In that sublime moment of flashing lights... Something stopped... The dark of the screens were out of tune with the words transmitted... For all to see... Everyone understood... Every eye saw? Every city read.... Every city knew....

Every advertising sign was hacked, every mobile device, every website, and every television station in town. It was not known how it was done, who it was, nor where it came from. All this, all this effort for someone to leave just one message.

"They used to say that back then evil was strong, it acted in every physical form of being. But today, we are more and more sure that evil acts differently, because we all know, and we don't have the courage to speak out, that today evil rules by exploiting our subjectivity."

"Do you guys believe in freedom?"

"Or have they been convinced to believe that it exists?"